A PRODUCT~~IVE~~ ~~MEMBER~~ OF SOCIETY

JERRY HUTCHINSON

A Product~~ive Member~~ of Society

Produced and printed by Stillwater River Publications.

Visit our website at
www.StillwaterPress.com
for more information.

First Stillwater River Publications Edition.

ISBN: 978-1-965733-02-8

1 2 3 4 5 6 7 8 9 10
Written by Jerry Hutchinson.
Cover image provided by Jerry Hutchinson.
Illustrations by Jerry Hutchinson.
Published by Stillwater River Publications,
West Warwick, RI, USA.

I would like to thank my bestie, Tina Westemeier, for helping me through the roughest time of my life. She has been a beacon of positivity and hope. With her unwavering moral compass, she has played a pivotal role in turning this book into a reality. I cannot thank you enough.

A special thanks to the two people that have been in my corner from day one; Mom and Dad, I cannot ever thank you enough.

Dedicated to my grandmother.
She will be missed.

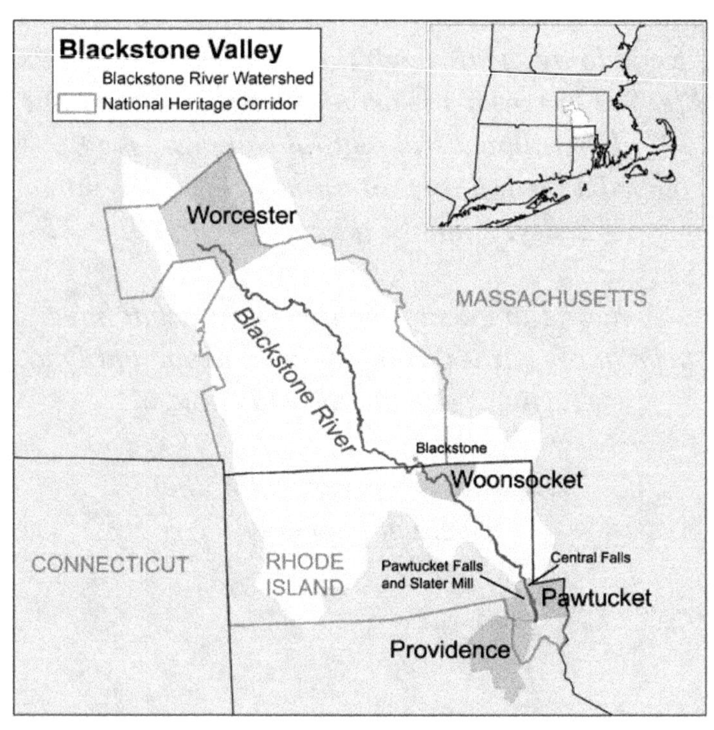
Blackstone Valley
Blackstone River Watershed
National Heritage Corridor
Worcester
MASSACHUSETTS
Blackstone River
Blackstone
Woonsocket
CONNECTICUT
RHODE
ISLAND
Pawtucket Falls
and Slater Mill
Central Falls
Pawtucket
Providence

The Blackstone River is a river in the United States that flows through the states of Massachusetts and Rhode Island. It is 48 mi (77 km) long and drains into the Seekonk tidal river at Pawtucket, Rhode Island. The original Native American name for the river was the "Kittacuck," which meant "the great tidal river." The "Kittacuck" used to be plentiful with salmon and lamprey in pre-colonial and colonial times. Its long history of industrial use has caused significant pollution, with the United States Environmental Protection Agency describing it as "the most polluted river in the country because of high concentrations of toxic sediments."

"Blackstone River." Wikipedia.
https://en.wikipedia.org/wiki/Blackstone_River.

CHAPTER ONE

Providence, Rhode Island c. 1998

I'm stuck in this damn elevator with this prick again. I swear, if he opens his mouth, I'm going to kill him.

He is a scrawny, disheveled man, looking of yesterday's used diaper. I have had the displeasure of being in his presence one too many times. His idiotic attempts at a conversation have usually started with, "Some weather, eh?" or "How about those Red Sox?" He never gets the subtle hints that I am not interested in his stupid small talk during what feels like a lifetime in this godforsaken vertical machine.

The elevator is dimly lit, like a noir movie. The single, long fluorescent bulb above us continues to blink from any movement of the elevator's contents or the stop and start at any floor. The smell is like a urinal at The Living Room night club.

He is standing to my left, both of us pressed against the back wall. My eyes forward as if there were something of importance in front of me, a clip of *The Big Lebowski* perhaps. Anything to take my mind off this asshole.

And then it happened…

"Did you see the game yesterday?'

HOLY SHIT! I knew it! He couldn't resist; he couldn't keep his big trap shut! Being a Red Sox fan (it was a mortal sin to be from New England and not be a Red Sox or Pats fan) I assumed that he was talking about the Sox and the Yanks' last night as it is off season for football.

"The Red Sox were wicked hot, on a three-game streak. Nomah is phenomenal!"

Fucking Nomah?! He obviously is related to Garciaparra! Idiot. Today is the day I'm going to finally kill this sonofabitch!

With my right hand, I grabbed the nonstandard, 9-inch, high carbon stainless steel survival blade with its 4.7-inch dual-edge knife, strapped to my left side underneath my black leather jacket. In a single instant I turned to face him and shoved the blade straight up under his chin and through the roof of his mouth, undoubtedly piercing into his pea-size brain. I held it there for a second or two and looked him dead in the eyes. His were of shock and horror. Mine? Well, they were just mine, intent and commanding. Giving him a final chance to see me, Death, to which he had every bit coming. This is not the first time I have looked into the eyes of my enemy, probably won't be the last.

As I pulled my knife out of his head, the spark seemed to disappear from his eyes as he dropped lifeless to the floor. I cleaned my knife on his cheap shirt and put it back in its place.

I returned to my statuesque position feeling a great sense of serenity.

A few seconds later the elevator stopped, and the door opened.

"Well, have a good day," were his final words as he exited.

The doors closed again.

Yeah…

Tomorrow.

I'll *definitely* kill that prick tomorrow.

STATISTICS WILL TELL YOU THAT THE ONE PERSON THAT CAN either make or break your day would be your significant other. My girl, Francine, used to make my days with her smile. She had a kiss that would melt the polar caps and a soft embrace that would calm the most savage of beasts. Now, many years later, after battles won and lost, she sucks the life right out of me like a demon vampire. Cold and lifeless.

This morning was no different. Being under a shit ton of stress over the increased workload, my doctor recommended I be put on an anti-frikin-anxiety med, Ativan. It works great, takes the edge off. However, the side effect is a decreased sex drive. The lack of ability to please your girl in bed takes a toll on your soul. Makes you hate the world. Hate yourself.

Well, she has grabbed onto this bomb and likes to light the fuse and drop it on my lap every damn chance she gets. Like it's her one single goal in life.

"What the fuck is wrong with you? Your dick broken?"

"I'm just dealing with a lot right now," I stated in my cowering best.

"You're fucking dealing with a lot?! What the fuck do you think I do? Sit around all day waiting for you to come home?"

"I'm sure that you don't."

"Damn right I don't!"

"Look, just give me a chance to figure this out."

"Well, you better figure it out quick, I'm sick of this shit!"

If the president of the goddamn United fucking States had to deal with this shit every morning I'm sure he would have sent this country into a nuclear war a long time ago!

THE ELEVATOR STARTED TO MOVE AGAIN. IN THE FEW MOMENTS I had before my stop I decided to inventory my gun and ammunition. This procedure is routinely done every morning during coffee and Tony Petrarca's forecast, but I derive comfort from the random check. The Glock 19's magazine was full, but I always carried a spare, just for that random asshole that didn't go down in my first fifteen rounds.

The elevator jolted to a final stop. Overshooting my floor (as usual) it crept down until it finally rested. I gave an audible snicker. "Piece of junk."

The doors opened and I took the first step off. Scanning the room, I counted at least a dozen people.

I raised my gun, and in a matter of seconds blew the face off the first three sorry asses that were closest to me. Poor fucks didn't know what hit them. After that it was chaos. Everyone else was either running to the stairway or hiding under their desks. I started to pick off the runners like I was shooting ducks in a row.

"HEY, DOC!"

"Oh, hey Jimmy."

"I have a lead on the guy you've been after. I thought you should check it out."

"Yeah, sure. How's the wife?"

"Doing great, Doc. Getting bigger every day."

Everyone called me Doc around here. In my early days Jack Daniels was very easy to remember, especially because I didn't mind having a drink or two.

However, one time, when I was serving a warrant with my former partner, the situation went bad quick. We knocked at this gorgeous house on the East Side. Why the perp was in this rich neighborhood? We figured that he was either hiding from us or hiding from the bad guys seeing as he was supposed to be testifying the next day against a drug kingpin. He was the key witness.

When the door opened a sweet looking old lady asked, "May I help you?"

Probably his grandmother.

Just then we saw our witness race across the long hall towards the back door. We yelled for him to stop but, probably figuring we were not the good guys, he then started firing on us with a pissant .32. My partner fired back, and the guy fell to the floor. We ran over to him as the old lady was screaming for help. I saw that my partner had shot him through the chest. Knowing he had to testify, I ripped open his shirt. Blood sprayed in my face. The bullet went through his lung causing a sucking chest

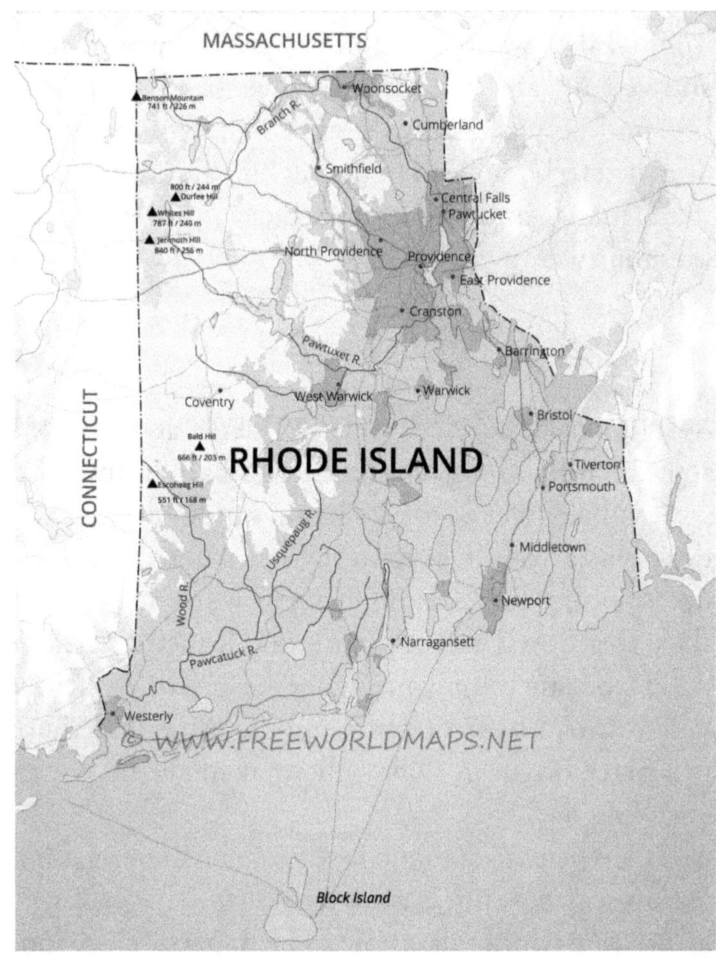

wound. Using my military training, I felt around for the guy's wallet. Grabbing his I.D., I covered the hole with it and then I turned the guy on his side so he could breathe better. He was losing a lot of blood even though I kept pressure on the wound.

Luckily, within minutes, Providence rescue showed up and took over. They say I saved his life, and he was able to testify the next day, albeit attached to an oxygen tank. Fuckin idiot. They gave me a medal and the name "Doc"; they gave the kingpin twenty years.

JIMMY IS A YOUNG DETECTIVE. GREEN AS THEY COME. BUT HE WAS resourceful and not too much of a pain in the ass.

I walked over to my desk and sat down. Jimmy's desk was a couple over to my left where he picked up a piece of paper and headed toward me. He put the paper down in front of me and leaned in a little.

He began telling me what he heard in a low voice. "So, I heard from a good source that there is a place down in Olneyville that might be worth checking out."

His whispering made it seem that this was a big fuckin secret. Truth is everyone knew. This case was all anyone could talk about. The papers, television, goddamn internet for Christ's sake! I've even had some dipshit reporter stick his microphone in my face for a comment. He's another one on my kill list for tomorrow.

The chief has been up my ass about this case since I inherited it from the last detective that was getting close to finding this guy. Too close. He wound up fish food in the Blackstone.

The chief figured I could handle a case like this. After serving most of my time with the marines in Iraq during the Gulf War, I've seen my fair share of death and dismemberment. People getting blown to shit and not being able to find all their body parts. Maybe a couple fingers here, part of a head over there, and a splatter of blood was all that was left. This case brought me right back to all of that. The smell of death was the worst part. Something I hoped to never experience again, but it follows me. Haunts me like a relentless ghost. It never sleeps and never gets buried. It feeds on shit like this...

And it's always hungry.

JIMMY'S INFORMATION WAS NOTHING MORE THAN A "SOMEONE that may have seen something." He was a good kid, and I didn't want to brush him off, so I gave him a chance to go and check it out. See if he can get something a little more concrete. It will keep him out of harm's way but keep him involved. I felt some responsibility for him because he looked up to me. Stupid kid.

"I won't let you down, Doc!" Energetic little prick.

"Just ask questions. Don't piss anyone off. You got me?"

"Sure thing Doc. Don't worry about me."

As soon as he said that I started to worry.

"HEY DOC, YOUR EX IS ON LINE TWO."

Detective Johnson, she was a looker. Mid-thirties, blonde, and sweet as an angel. She usually gets the hooker details to lure in the johns.

"And she sounds pissed. Did you miss another payment?"

"Thanks Johnson." (Bitch)

"JACK!?" Oh shit.

"Yeah, what's up?"

"I'll tell you what's up, it's your daughter."

"Really?? What's wrong with Cristina?"

There is one person in this whole rotten, damned world that I would give my life for and that is my daughter, Cristina. She just turned eight this past December twenty-fourth. A terrible birthday for a kid, the day before Christmas. I always tried to make it special for her. Whatever she wanted. She wanted a bike; she got a bike. She wanted a drum set; I got her a drum set. That was a nice present for her mother too. Meanest fuckin woman you will ever cross. Fuck her.

"I'll tell you what is wrong with her. She has holes in her school shoes! Are you okay sending her to school with holes in her shoes? Because I'm not! You better send me some money, Jack. Because if you miss another child support payment, I'm taking you to court to have your visitation cut!"

"I only get to see her every other weekend as it is!"

"I don't give a shit, Jack."

I'm not sure if she can do that but I know some guys on the force that have missed a payment or two and ended up getting fucked. The courts don't give a shit what your job is. You don't pay, you're a deadbeat dad and you get fucked.

"Look, Monica, things have been a little difficult lately. This case has me upside down. I promise I will get you that payment by the end of the day tomorrow. Just give me till tomorrow." A total lie but it bought me another day.

"That's it, Jack. You have until tomorrow to get me that money or you can kiss your daughter goodbye!" (*Click*)

There are not enough foul words in the Webster's fuckin dictionary to describe the Evil Being that this woman has become. This bitch of a person is holding my daughter's life hostage over a few measly dollars.

Where did I put those goddamn pills???

After I gently placed the phone down (*slam*!), I jumbled my way through a couple of desk drawers (damn desk is always a mess) until I found my prescription. The label read "Ativan 0.5 mg. Take 1 pill 3 times a day as needed." I tend to focus on the "as needed" part; fuck the rest, and my dick.

"DOC." I LOOKED UP AND SAW THE CHIEF WAS CALLING ME.

This goddamn morning just won't quit!

He was using his index and middle fingers in a kind of mini "come here" wave. I took a deep breath and pushed my chair back then got up and started making my way through the maze of desks toward his office.

The chief, or Bobby as I like to call him, was about my age. We went through the academy together. Our careers took different paths; mine was a beat man, and his was of politics. Which meant that we had a common ground, but one that I should tread softly on. Should.

He went to sit behind his desk and left his door slightly open for me, which was far from his usual "shut up and do not disturb me with bullshit" manner.

"What's up Chief?"

Over the years, from sitting on his ass, he has

struggled with his weight. He started out a slim, not too tall recruit. Now he is a short, chubby, balding fuck. His portly stature is mildly shrouded from behind his desk. He needs a bigger desk.

"Sit down, Jack." Number one, sitting down means that you are not going to be leaving after a thirty-second ass-chewing. And number two, he called me by my name. Neither of these are signs I will be getting shown pictures from his oldest daughter's wedding, which I was not fucking invited to by the way.

In a sarcastic undertone I decided to use the same vernacular he chose.

"What can I do for you, Bobby?"

He gave me a small, unsavory smirk.

"Jack, how's it going with this case? Any leads?"

"Sure. I just sent Jimmy out to poke around some trash cans. Hopefully he can find some maggots. Why?"

"I've been on the phone with the DA all morning. They are getting itchy trigger fingers and if you don't find someone that they can point their guns at soon, they are going to be pointing them at me, which means I will be pointing mine at you. Understand?"

"Sure Bobby." Prick. "Anything else?"

He truly hated it when people didn't call him chief. He settled forward in his chair as he placed his elbows on his desk and started massaging his hands. Dipshit.

"Yeah, JACK." He really emphasized my name as a show of how annoyed he was. "I got a call from a Miss Monica Modene. Ring any bells?" He knew very well who the fuck she was.

"Vaguely."

"Well, she tells me that you missed another child support payment. That's three this year. Seeing as it is only April, if you don't start making this right, the department will have to take it out of your ass. We don't tolerate—"

"I got it, CHIEF. Is that it?"

"Yes." He turned his attention to some paperwork on his desk, so I got up to leave. But before I made it through his door, he had to get one more shit dump out of his mouth. "Hey, Jack..."

I stopped and turned.

I pulled on my holster so hard I nearly tore a hole in my shirt! Before he could mutter a fucking word, I aimed my gun at his fat, sweaty forehead and unloaded a single shot. He was dead before I put my gun back in its home under my shoulder.

"Don't fuck this case up."

Asshole.

I CIRCLED AROUND TO MY DESK, SAT DOWN, AND BEGAN TO CON-template the *dickhead's* "pep talk." The fact that my ex had called him put her on a new lower level of shit.

This is one of the highest profile cases this damn department has ever seen, and he is expecting me to come up with answers less than a week into it. The fact was that I didn't have any true leads to follow.

Detective Silva was a good man. The only good that came out of his death was the benefits to his widow. But when he got whacked, the Blackstone took him and most of the case with him. The only scent he left was full of mud. That's why the chief is following me so close. One dead cop is one too many by anyone's books.

I needed a drink.

I STOOD UP AND WENT INTO THE BREAK AREA. NOT A *ROOM* because it used to be an office until maintenance had taken the door off and hung up a sign that said, "break ~~room~~ *area.*" My guess is that if they called it a room, they would have to give it to some "deserving" desk-pusher. Fact is we needed someplace to put our coffee pot and walking into some jackass's office to make coffee would just be awkward.

The room was empty, to my satisfaction, so I

picked up the pot and poured a cup. The creamer the department sprung for was these little fucking cups that held a drop of cream. Whoever came up with these things was an idiot! Probably a rich idiot, but an idiot, nonetheless. I used seven of them.

I took my coffee and went over to the only window in the room. The panes were just clear enough to peak through. They were old and shit-stained with years of cigarettes being puffed on by cops that wanted to look just like Detective Michael "Mick" Belker from *Hill Street Blues*.

Squinting, I watched the people walking along the street like it was a movie dedicated to their monotonous lives. I felt dirty.

Providence was not like it used to be. The first time "Buddy" Cianci was mayor, dirtbags like the one I am chasing wouldn't last a second. Everyone knew that there was backroom shit going on, but we accepted it because there was a code. Kind of like that great fucking movie *Casino*. As long as the money kept coming in, and things stayed quiet, there were no issues. But once you start making too much noise you end up like Joe Pesci and his brother: at the bottom of a ditch in the middle of nowhere. We were all glad that Buddy won another term but this time it was different. There were a few years' gap in between his terms which seemed to erupt in chaos. Too much damn political correctness, if you ask me.

I started to lose myself in the chaos of the streets. Remembering my childhood and how some friends and I would ride our Huffy bikes down from Pawtucket into Providence. We would grab a burger from Haven Brothers and sit on the city hall stairs. There was an occasional homeless drunk but for the most part we felt safe. Funny how shit changes.

"HEY, DOC. SAUSAGE IS ON LINE ONE."

By the time I turned around no one was there but I knew it was Sanchez. Ass. Just because Jimmy's last name was Dean a few of the guys made it into a joke. Unfortunately, it stuck. I knew Jimmy didn't care for it, so I never used it. Besides, maybe his parents named him after James Dean, The Rebel Without a Cause. But what the hell did I know? Maybe they loved sausage or conceived him on the breakfast table.

I threw the shit coffee in the trash and made it over to my desk.

"What's up, Jimmy?" I could hear Spanish music and street noise.

"Doc. I'm down in Olneyville." That explained the music.

"What's going on?"

"Well, I went to South Providence and talked to the guy that I told you about. He told me about this crack cocaine dealer in Olneyville and gave me an address. I'm outside now and there is a lot of activity. Do you want me to check it out?"

"Jimmy, you just sit tight, and I will be there in five minutes. You got me?"

"Yeah, Doc, I got you. But you should hurry, it looks like they are packing up."

"Shit! What's your location?"

"I'm on the corner of Dike and Troy."

I put the phone down and jetted for the stairs.

After the elevator ride earlier, I didn't want to chance getting trapped with another ass.

My 1964 Ford mustang convertible looked like a piece of shit. The body had patch marks on both rear quarters, a dent in the driver door (which left it inoperable), and the ragtop looked like, well, a rag. The color was a faded blue. But under the hood I could keep up with the best. Even though being a Special Victims Unit detective meant using a department vehicle, they didn't give me any shit, probably because I totaled a cruiser by sending it into the Woonasquatucket River. I had a perfectly good reason for doing it, but I didn't have time to wonder about it now. I just had to get to Jimmy.

It was a beautiful spring day, a little warmer than average, so the top was already down from my ride in this morning, which made it easy for me to just hop in. I threw the key in the ignition and started her up. She gave a small knock, which was more like a backfire, then I put her in gear and sped off.

Olneyville was only a few minutes' drive from the station but culturally it was another country. It has a population of about seven thousand with the majority being Hispanic. At least half of the occupants are considered low-income, which basically means that the crime rate is unbelievable. These people will stab you for a fucking nickel.

Driving down Westminster Street, nearing the

turn onto Troy, a familiar smell surrounded me. Aside from street trash, cannabis, and a burnt-out Burger King, I could smell the only thing that ever really enticed me to come down here: New York System wieners. Deliciously made on a guy's arm, a dog, meat sauce, some onion, and topped with celery salt. Throw it down with some coffee milk and I'll be a happy guy. After I see Jimmy, I may just take him for a couple.

Making the turn onto Troy Street, my sense of smell was forgotten, and I heard a sound I knew all too well: gunfire.

I could see Jimmy. He had taken cover behind a vehicle and was returning fire to a building on the corner. I skidded to a stop behind him, put it in park, and got a sharp burning in my left arm as I jumped out of the passenger door. I knew I had been hit but I also knew it wasn't serious.

"Jimmy! What the hell is going on?"

"Doc! They were about to leave so I asked them a couple of questions to stall them."

"Well, I guess you got your fucking answer!"

I poked my head up to see what the situation was. It was the J Shatz Ceramic building at 46 Dike Street. The black-and-white building stuck out like a fucking sore thumb among this redbrick mill area.

"Jimmy, call this in, dammit!"

While Jimmy called for backup, I popped a couple off into the front window of the place. Right next to the window was a garage door that was partially open and someone there was firing at us, as well as another from the other side of the building. I'm guessing there to be about three of them.

There was a large delivery truck across the street from them that I could get behind and get a better vantage point from.

"Jimmy, you stay here and cover me! And wait for backup!"

"Sure, Doc."

I counted to three and Jimmy and I acted together. He popped a few rounds as I ran across the street and got behind the truck. I threw a couple rounds as I ran but didn't see where they went.

Behind the truck I saw the guy in the garage door and got a clean shot on him easy. After he fell, the guy on the side of the building had disappeared. I tried to see where he went just as the guy in the window got off a shot, but not at me. I looked to where he was shooting, and the world seemed to have stopped rotating.

Nothing moved.

Not even Jimmy.

He must have felt that they were retreating after the first guy fell and the other took off, so he started advancing.

Now he lay motionless in the middle of the street.

I raised my Glock and unloaded it into the window as I ran across the street. My back against the building, I swung my head into the garage to get a look at how bad I hit the fucker, but just then a black van came blazing out. If I hadn't pulled back quick enough it would have taken my head clean off.

I threw another mag in and shot off a few rounds at the back as it sped off and went down a service road, then out of sight.

Damn!

They got away…

Jimmy!

I ran over to him and turned him onto his back. He was alive, barely. The bullet missed his vest and got him in the neck. I put pressure on it, but he was mortally bleeding. I knew in my gut that he was not going to make it.

"Hey, Doc," he softly murmured.

"I told you to wait for backup!"

"You can fix me, right Doc?"

"Sure, Jimmy. Sure."

He gave a small smile as sirens flooded.

His eyes fell, lifeless.

"I told you to wait!"

MY LEFT ARM WAS COVERED IN BLOOD. ALTHOUGH THE BULLET grazed me, the bloody mess made it look worse than it was. The EMT was wrapping me up just as they were taking Jimmy and putting him in the back of another ambulance. They were trying to get a pulse as the doors closed. The siren went on and they drove off.

I knew he was not coming back.

But they had to try.

"JACK!"

"Bobby, not now."

"It's Chief, and it's right fucking NOW!"

The chief had left his usual position from behind his desk to make a special appearance. Lucky us.

The EMT had finished wrapping me up, so I examined my jacket. It had a hole in the left arm that wasn't there this morning. I shook my head in disgust then put it on. Tough to get a decent jacket in this town. Had to travel up to Emerald Square Mall in Attleboro for this one.

"What the fuck happened here, Jack?"

In a tired, exhausted tone, I groaned "Jimmy followed up on a lead. By the time I got on scene he was engaged in a firefight. We called for backup. I shot one but the others got away."

"And now Jimmy is dead!"

Hearing that was like a lightning bolt jetting through my veins. Words came out of my mouth so fast and driven that I was surprised he didn't fall over.

"I know Jimmy's fucking dead!"

Ours eyes locked in a moment. He knew to leave me the fuck alone. Then I walked away.

"Where are you going, Jack?"

"Cranston."

Jimmy lived there.

So did his pregnant wife.

THE MODEST HOME WAS IN THE EDEN PARK AREA. SMALL YARD, blue shutters, one-car garage, and an American flag waving off the front above the Munroe Dairy box on the stoop. Something about what a new detective could afford.

His wife is a nurse at Butler Hospital but was on maternity leave. She was due in five days. Jimmy was always very proud to be a budding father which meant that he was forthcoming with every detail of his wife's progress. I didn't mind. Was nice to hear of some goodness in this shitty world.

I parked on the street in front of the house and walked up the flagstone to the front door. After I rang the doorbell, I heard a sweet, young voice.

"Hang on a minute!"

A couple of seconds later the door opened. Jimmy's wife, Lucy, was in sweats and looking like her belly was going to burst at any moment.

"Oh, hey, Jack. I was just doing some last-minute baby room cleaning. Want to make sure everything is just right."

"Uh, Lucy, may I come in?"

"Of course, yeah. Everything alright? Where's Jimmy?"

I stepped in and closed the door.

CHAPTER TWO

I stayed with Lucy until her mother arrived. She took the death of her husband as any caring woman would. I told her if she needed anything to let me know. As far as the baby was concerned, the state has a decent survivor's package. Never enough to replace the loss if you ask me.

In my time I have watched more friends die than anyone should. I have learned to deal with it, almost too coldly. But there is nothing in the world worse than telling a loved one the news. Fucking brutal, but I wanted to tell her before some unknown-to-her cop came to her door. Jimmy would have wanted it that way.

I MUDDLED OVER THE MORNING AS I DROVE BACK TO THE STATION. Some shit day so far. I gave some thought to my next move as I pulled in.

"Jack."

I no sooner make it to my desk when Chief Dick called. I gave him a side glance. He gave me the two-finger shit again. Hell.

I went into his office as I did not long ago, but this time he wasn't alone.

"Jack, this is Special Agent Rogers. He will be assisting you with this case."

"The FB-friggin-I? Bobby, Chief, what the hell is going on?"

"Jack, one dead cop is more than enough. Now we have two and the agency feels they need to step in, and so do I."

"This is bullshit!"

"You WILL get Agent Rogers up to speed and he WILL assist you. Copy?"

I took one look at Rogers. He was a pissant, suited, stiff-ass. If the chief thinks I am going to let this guy ASSIST me, he can kiss *my* ass.

"Uh, Agent Rogers, can you step outside for a moment?" The chief motioned his chubby fingers toward the door.

"Sure." He kept his stupid eyes on me as he exited the room.

As soon as the door closed, I started.

"Bobby, what the hell?"

"Jack, just sit down a minute. I had no choice in the matter. These guys have taken out two detectives. That shit travels fast. This guy showed up just before you got here."

Sonuvabitch. I sat down, reluctantly.

"Sorry, Jack, but my hands are tied. I know Jimmy was your friend."

"He was a good cop, dammit! You know that!" I was getting even more angry.

He raised his voice to mock mine. "Yes, he was, but he was out checking on a lead that YOU sent him on. The people upstairs wanted your badge, but I got them to back off!"

"I appreciate that, Chief." Okay, that got me speaking semi-respecfully as I eased back into my chair.

"Well, don't appreciate it too much because if you don't come up with something soon my word won't be worth shit."

I thought about it for a second or two then stood up to leave thinking he was finished. But, as before, he had to get a final word in.

"Jack," I paused but didn't turn around, "try not to get him killed."

Kill him? Shit. He wasn't on today's kill list, but it is early and I'm sure he will magically materialize on it later; right now I had a call to make.

I LEFT THE CHIEF'S OFFICE AND WALKED RIGHT PAST ROGERS ON the way to my desk. I could feel him following me. I sat down and he stopped in front of me.

"Look, I know you are invested in—"

I cut him off. "Hey, there is a desk right there."

I pointed to the vacant desk in front of me. It was Silva's. No one had claimed it yet, probably due to shit superstition.

"If you are going to be tailing me you might as well take a seat."

He looked at the desk with a questionable gaze. The desk was old and covered with a new, thin layer of dust. It was made of a heavy metal and painted a putrid green that was chipped at every corner and faded on all the drawers. It was heavily used, and it showed. Rogers looked around to see if there was a different one. No such luck.

"The coffee room is over there." I pointed at the break area. "Why don't you go grab a cup? I have to make a call."

He could tell that I was just trying to get rid of him, so he just crossed his arms and stood still. Fucking statue.

"Look I have to call my girl. You get a coffee and when you get back, I'll tell you what you want to know. Deal?"

He smirked a little then conceded and walked away. A man of few fucking words. At least he has something going for him.

It's not like I lied to him. I was going to call Francine, just not right away.

I opened my second drawer and grabbed a cell phone that I snatched from a perp during a drug bust some years ago. I use it when I don't want people to know that it's me calling.

I dialed the number.

A soft voice answered.

"Hello?"

"Hey Monica. It's me, Jack."

Her demeanor changed immediately.

"Jesus Christ, Jack. What do you want?"

"I was just hoping I could say hi to Cristina." It was just past two and I knew she would be home from school.

"She's busy playing in the backyard with some friends from school. And I have company. Try calling later."

"Maybe I can come by later to see her?"

She didn't answer.

"I heard your friend got shot today. How are you doing, *Jack*?"

She didn't give a shit. She was implying shit about my state of mind and not wanting me to bring my problems to our daughter.

"I'm fine. Can I come see her?"

"Just call later. Not after nine."

Disgusted and feeling like a hole was in my chest from not being able to see Cristina, I growled, "Fine."

She hung up.

I put the phone down and reached in my top drawer for another fucking pill. I took one out and placed it on my tongue and just swallowed it with whatever spit I had.

To say that I completely fucking hated her would not begin to explain how I felt.

I looked over and could see the silhouette of Rogers still in the break area, so I decided to make another call.

I picked up the phone and dialed.

The man on the other end did not answer with the softness of Monica.

"What?!"

I responded with the same attitude but in a whisper. "What do you mean, what? What the fuck is going on?"

"Hey asshole, don't press me. Don't give me any reason to break our deal. You don't mean shit to me."

"Look, you just follow through on your end of the bargain. Okay?"

No answer. I could hear just a few people talking and a scream before the line went dead.

"Fuck!"

"Sounded like an intense phone call. You and your girl good?"

I looked up and saw Rogers leaning against *his* desk and I wondered how long he had been standing there.

"Yeah. We're good."

CHAPTER THREE

We had made it down to my car and were just pulling away from the station.

"You hungry?" It was now about two thirty and aside from a shit cup of coffee, I don't remember eating breakfast.

"I can eat." Rogers waved me on.

His first look at my car, I was used to: the pause, then the look of confusion.

"We're riding in this…thing?"

"Well, I am. If you want to follow me…" I didn't finish on purpose. In fact, if he took his own car, it would be easier to lose him.

He answered with a sort of grunted distaste, "No, no. That's okay."

He watched me jump over my broken door and started to think he had to do the same.

"That door opens. Feel free to use it, or jump in. I don't care." Chump probably didn't want to get his suit dirty.

We started down Atwells Ave. I had a craving for a good pizza, so I decided to go to Caserta's.

I'm not one for small talk, but I can't stand silence. Makes me uneasy and I start thinking of ways I have had to kill people. My doc says I have PTSD from the service. Fuck he knows. Probably never served a day in the shit.

I turned on the radio. HJY was playing the Stones—"Sympathy for the Devil." "Pleased to meet you, hope you guess my name." I started singing along.

It was a short drive but with the stiff it felt like a goddamn road trip across the state. When I finally parked and shut off the car, he spoke a single word.

"Interesting."

What the fuck does that mean? This guy was about to be my next victim. I gave him a shitty look and, luckily for him, he got out before I could reach my knife.

We walked in and sat at a booth towards the back. It gave us a little privacy as I am sure he was hoping for. Easier for him to hear details of my case.

The waitress came over. "Welcome to Caserta's. What can I get you?"

I gave him a commanding look, like "I got

this." "We'll have a large cheese with pepperoni and mushrooms. Oh, and he will have a Wimpy Skimpy. And two coffee milks please." She smiled and walked away.

"Wimpy Skippy?"

"Yeah, you'll like it."

He didn't seem amused.

"Alright, Jack, or is it, Doc?" he started.

"Doc is just what the guys at the station call me. Jack is what my ex-wife calls me. So why don't you go with Detective Daniels."

"Okay, Detective, what do you have for me?"

"Well, why don't you tell me what you know, and I will try to fill in the gaps for you?" I decided to play a little cat and mouse with him.

"Well, about four months ago, girls between the ages of seven and ten started disappearing."

"Not overly unusual but go on."

"According to our records, after the fourth girl went missing, the other three started showing up. One by one. Each was bound and had their face meticulously carved off. As if done with the precision of a surgeon."

Our coffee milks arrived. I had a refreshing gulp. He looked at his for a moment, then took a sip. He probably came over from the Midwest where their coffee milk consists of a cup of coffee with a glass of milk. Great. A fucking redneck farm boy.

After she walked away, he continued, "After your Detective Silva was killed, five more girls went missing. All but two have been found. All in the same manner as the others."

"Sounds like you have the gist."

"Yeah, well, I need some more information. Like the places where they were found, for starters."

"Along the Blackstone River" *as if he knows where that is* "which means that they could be getting dumped in just about any city or town north of Providence."

"I would like to take a look at the coroner records. Talk to the families."

"You think that is a wise idea? I mean, coroner yes, but to talk to the families and put them through it all over again?"

"Maybe if I can just look over the reports."

The pizza came over.

The waitress put the Wimpy in front of him. He looked at it, then looked at me.

I gave him a little chuckle. "Hey, it's a spinach and black olive calzone."

He either didn't seem to care for it, or he just smelt his own fart. Same look either way.

"Where are you from, Rogers?"

"Clovis, New Mexico."

"You don't have much of a southern accent."

I picked up a slice of pizza and took a bite. He pushed the Wimpy aside and grabbed a slice.

"My parents were military. My mother was originally from the Boston area and my father was from Florida. Both were stationed at Cannon Air Force base, just outside of Clovis. I was in Braintree visiting a sick uncle when I got the call to come down here."

"I was wondering how you got here so quickly."

"Yeah, I hardly ever come up this way. Not much family except for my uncle and, above all, the weather here is too cold."

He sounded like a typical eighty-year-old snowbird.

Although his mouth was full of heavenly pizza, he continued, "Since we are on the subject, where are you from?"

I gave him a Look. Seriously?

"Good ole Rhode Island, born and bred. Since my divorce, I put up in a small apartment on North Bend Street in Pawtucket." I took another slice.

"Divorced? Sorry to hear it," he said with that country "I really care" look.

"Hey, don't be. She was a great woman the first year of our marriage, but then became mean as a snake."

"Women." He shook his head in a disapproving fashion. "Any kids?'

"Just a daughter, Cristina." She's the only girl I ever truly loved. "You married? Kids?"

"No, sir," he quickly answered. "The Bureau is the only love for me at the moment."

What a dipshit.

We finished up the pizza and I asked the waitress to wrap the Wimpy. I'll probably eat it later tonight when I wake up from a sweat-soaked dream.

We got back in the car just as he asked about the shooting this morning.

"Why don't we head over there," I answered plainly. "It was just down the street a bit."

I turned the radio up to stop his questioning and to hear Axel Rose singing, "She takes me away to that special place, and if I stare too long, I'd probably break down and cry."

CHAPTER FOUR

We made our way to Troy Street then turned left. I could see Detective Sanchez and some beat cops.

Sanchez was heavily built with dark hair, of Native American descent and proud of it. He always wore a colorful vest or shirt and some sort of necklace that looked like he was just off the reservation. He had an inkling for forensics, and he always showed up at crime scenes. Even though he looks around for evidence, he sometimes mucks it up for the real forensics.

"Hey, Sanchez," I greeted him as we pulled up and hopped out of my car. He gave a small grin to see me climbing over my broken door.

The area was still taped off. I noticed the blood on the ground where Jimmy was laid out. I know it was dry, but it still looked as if someone could suck it up with a turkey baster and put it back into Jimmy's body. An old familiar chill from the other side of the world came over me.

"This is Rogers. He is from the Bureau and will be tagging along."

"I'd like to think of it as helping with the investigation," he said as he glanced to me and then back to Sanchez. "Nice to meet you."

They opted not to shake hands because Sanchez was wearing gloves, so they just gave a head bob. They looked like a couple of fucking five-year-old kids meeting at the playground for the first time. "You want to go on the swings?" "Okay." Idiots.

"You find anything?" I inquired.

"Aside from shell casings, not much. But forensics is inside."

I gave a quick scan of the outside of the building and noticed a couple of security cameras on its corners.

"Did you check the footage?" I pointed up at one of them.

"Not yet but I'll get on it. I'll let you know if I find anything."

"Thanks."

Rogers and I ambled over to the garage doorway where I stood just a few hours ago and almost lost my head. I paused for one more look at Jimmy's bloodstain in the middle of the street as if hoping that it wasn't true, then we went in.

Over the years I have gotten to know some of the crime scene investigators. They are usually very serious and take their job quite the same. However, George is not the normal forensic. If he ever found a face that was cut off, I can totally fucking see him putting it on and saying, "Clarice, I Do Wish We Could Chat Longer, But I'm Having an Old Friend for Dinner." Then stick his tongue through the hole and make a sucking sound.

"Hey, George," I called as we made our way through the maze of evidence numbers on the floor.

"Hey, Doc! I was wondering when you'd be coming by." George was always dressed in a lab coat, gloves, and a Hawaiian shirt. He was a character and a goofball, but a very smart one. He leaned into my ear and whispered, "Who's the stiff?"

"George, I would like to introduce you to one of the Bureau's finest. George, Rogers. Rogers, George."

George looked at Rogers quizzically. "FBI? What the hell? Must be getting desperate with this case."

"My words exactly. But let's not dig up old graves. Any luck with this place?"

From the outside, this place looked like another local business that was trying to make a statement while, all along, just doing the same shit that some other guy was doing, and probably charging more for it. Owning a business in this neighborhood gave a more literal meaning to cutthroat.

On the inside this place was quite elaborate. High ceilings, carpeting, lighting fixtures—all spelling M-O-N-E-Y. Why the hell they were in the middle of such a shit town? I could only imagine that it was just a front for drugs, or worse, and this was the spot to keep a low profile.

"The place was pretty cleaned out," George said while reaching in his pocket to pull out his usual Jolly Rancher. "But the back rooms are what I want you to take a look at."

"Lead the way." I gave him a smirk and a wave of my hand like a medieval gent.

While we were walking, George turned to Rogers. "You want a Rancher?"

And reached in his pocket and pulled out a red one to give to him.

"Oh, uh, yeah. Sure. Thanks."

George looked at me and started to giggle.

"What's funny?" said Rogers.

"Oh, he is just happy when people accept his candy," I said to Rogers, but that was a complete fucking lie. George's candy is always the THC kind. Sometimes he gives me a couple that I use to help sleep better.

Rogers opened his Rancher and put it in his

mouth. "Mmm, good. Thank you." He knocked it around in his teeth.

All three of us giggled for different reasons.

There were three rooms on either side of the hall off the main area. We went by the first on the left that looked like a normal office with a picture window looking out into the main area. The next room was on the right, filled with boxes neatly stacked, and was obviously used for storage of printing paper and business filings. George led us to the second door on the left. As we entered, I noticed that the room was empty except for two mattresses on the floor. No bedding. No pillows. Just mattresses.

George pulled an evidence bag out of his pocket. "And these were found attached to the eyehook above one of the beds."

The bag contained a short chain and a pair of handcuffs covered in what looked like bloody residue. I took the bag from George and looked at the cuffs. The initials were easy to see, and I knew immediately that there was a problem.

J P

I walked over to one wall where an eyehook was, examined it closer, and noticed some more dried blood on the wall with the word, "**HELP**," clearly written.

George then pulled out a second, smaller bag that contained what looked like hair. "Found these on each of the mattresses."

"Damn, George, nice job. How soon can you get them to the lab?"

"For you? Give me a few hours. We are still dusting some areas for prints and doing a final survey, but I'll call you."

"Thanks, George."

"Alright, Rogers, let's get out of his way."

Rogers and I started for the door when I turned around.

"Hey, George, you think I can have one or two Ranchers?"

He reached in his pocket and threw a couple to me.

"Thanks again."

Rogers gave a small wave and said thank you again to George as he pointed to the protuberance in his cheek. I smiled back at George. His returned smile was full of the same hidden meaning as mine.

AS WE EXITED THE BUILDING, I LOOKED AT MY WATCH AND REAL-ized I was losing track of time.

"Rogers, why don't you wait for me at the car? I have to make a phone call." I usually give Francine a call when I'm at lunch and seeing as numb nuts took up my lunch with his less than appealing company, I was running a little late.

"No problem. I hope it's better than the last time you talked to her," he referred to the shitty conversation he overheard but a short time ago at the precinct.

I thought for a second, then replied," Yeah, you and me both."

He walked past Sanchez to my car while I took a right out of the door and made it to the side of the building. Only a couple beat cops were there for traffic and safety purposes, although this place won't see many rubberneckers until this gets blasted on the six o'clock news. Channels 10 and 12 were already on scene and pressing for questions.

"Hey, Doc! What's the scoop?" one reporter yelled over to me.

The scoop is that I am going to shove that microphone up your ass!

I threw up my hand like I was stopping traffic and continued walking down the side of the building. I got far enough away that I considered it out of earshot and pulled out my cellphone. Not that I give a shit who heard my conversation, but I just wanted a little damn privacy.

The phone rang a few times, then Francine answered.

"Hello?" she answered in her sweet voice.

"Hi. How are you?"

"Just terrific." I could tell she was upset.

"Sorry I didn't call. I got held up at lunch with a Fed."

"Fed? Like FBI, Fed?"

"Yeah. After Jimmy's death this morning they sent me a friggin tagalong."

Her mood seemed to dissolve a little.

"That sucks, Jack."

"Sure does. Kid from out west. We are just leaving the scene."

"So, you think you will be home about five?" she changed the subject. "I have a new recipe I was hoping to try out on you tonight." She considered herself a chef. In actuality, she was an amateur cook, at best, but I would never admit it to her.

"I will try but probably not."

Her mood bounced back so fast that I was surprised my ear didn't get whiplash.

"What the fuck, Jack!"

And the line went dead.

Fucking pills are in my desk drawer.

I STARTED MY WAY BACK TO THE FRONT OF THE BUILDING. MORE attempts from the media. I wanted so bad to give them the finger, but I gave them the "halt" hand again.

When I turned the corner of the building and headed toward my car, I could see Rogers was sitting in my seat.

What the fuck?

As I got closer, I noticed that he was eating my Wimpy!

"Hey, what the hell are you doing?"

"Oh, hey, Jack. I just wanted to feel what this seat was like."

"No, asshat. Why are you eating my Wimpy?"

"I was hungry?" He gave me a look like a kid getting caught in the cookie jar. "And I should have taken your word for it. It's delicious!"

Jesus Christ. "Get in the other fucking seat."

As he made his way over the hump I was cursing and laughing to myself. Damn George!

CHAPTER FIVE

"Wow, this is awesome, I feel great!"

Jesus.

Rogers was doing the wave with his arm in the wind as we rode back to the station. I needed to do some work and I needed to get him out of my hair. I don't have the time to be babysitting. I decided to drop him somewhere safe so he wouldn't get into any trouble.

A few moments later we were over the 195 bridge and pulled up to a house in East Providence.

"Hey, Jack, what are we doing here?" he asked in a mellow tone.

"We are just going to say hi to a friend of mine."

"Aww." His face fell to resemble a puppy dog's. "That's so great that you have friends."

"Well, maybe you can be her friend too," I suggested as we got out of the car.

"Jack, do you really think so?"

"I sure do. Let's go say hello."

"Okay, Jack. Hello. Hello." He started greeting the plants as we made our way up the walk.

I'm going to kill George.

I knocked on the door and an attractive blonde answered.

"Wow!" Rogers said very out loud, eyeballing her up and down.

"Jack." She looked at him then at me. "What's going on?"

"Hi, Tiffany. I'm kind of in a bind and I was hoping you could look after my friend until he, um, returns to earth."

Rogers's attention switched to the windchime that was hanging near the door.

Tiffany was a former prostitute that I had busted years ago but I conveniently "lost the report" if she would agree to give me information about the streets when I needed it. She's been out of that business for a couple years now; went legit, and got her massage therapy license, or was it phlebotomy. I forget, but I do know that she stuck with what she knew best, the body. And quite a body!

"Come on in." The last thing she wanted was to

have her neighbors see a couple of sketchy looking guys at her door.

As we went in, she looked out to see if anyone had seen, then she quickly closed the door behind us. Rogers made his way to a fish tank and became obsessed with the neon tetras.

"What the hell is wrong with him?" she asked quietly.

"He got into some edibles. He shouldn't be too much trouble. I just need to lose him for a couple hours."

"He looks like a tight-ass."

"He's a Fed from the Midwest."

"Well, that explains it."

"Can you help me out?"

"I guess. But it's going to cost you."

"What'll it be this time?"

"I'm having a problem with one of my neighbors. Just come by about midnight and you'll see."

"Deal. Thanks Tiffany." I gave her a kiss on the cheek.

"Hey, that will cost you too."

We both laughed a little.

I went over to Rogers. "Hey, this is Tiffany," I said as I grabbed his shoulder and peeled him away from the fish tank.

He looked at me and smiled, then looked at her. "Oh, hello. Have we met?"

"Ah, no. Hello, Rogers. Nice to meet you." They shook hands.

"Are we friends now?"

"We sure are. Why don't you come over here and have a seat and I'll make you some coffee milk." She led him toward the couch.

"Oh, do I like coffee milk?"

"I'll...see you in a little while, Rogers," I said to him as I made for the door, but I don't think his ears were hearing anything else except for what Tiffany was saying.

CHAPTER SIX

It was midafternoon, almost four, as I walked into the station. Without Rogers, I was able to sneak to my desk undetected, or so I thought. As I sat down and shoved my chair in, I heard a familiar voice.

"Doc," the chief hailed me like a taxi, "c'mon in here a minute." He wanted me to come to his office, but I was nearing my dumbass limit. I didn't want to be bothered by his nonsense right now, and besides, I didn't want him to start asking about Rogers. So, I picked up the phone and dialed his extension.

"Chief, I have some work going on here that is on a deadline. Can I get back to you later?"

"Jack, the DA is up my ass, as well as the commissioner, and the press. Can you just give me something? Anything?"

Damn puppet.

"Sure, I have something, but I need to make a call first to confirm. Can you give me a few minutes?"

"Okay, Jack. Just a few minutes. Oh, how is Rogers making out?"

"*What's that?*" I made like someone was saying something to me. "*Okay.*"

"Alright, Chief, I have to go. I'll get back to you in a bit. Bye." I hung the phone up quickly.

It's not like the fat-ass couldn't stand up and look out his mini-blinded windows to confirm whether I was talking to anyone or not, but I betted on his usual laziness.

I turned on my antiquated desktop computer. The department fell short on the budget a few years back and we lost our newer upgrades.

I looked at the clock. The warming up and logging in was going to take a couple of minutes so I decided to try my daughter again. I didn't want to use my confiscated phone too much. The department didn't know it, but they were paying its bill. So, this time I used my desk phone.

I dialed Monica's phone.

Because of me, she was likely screening her calls. It rang several times before the answering machine picked up. It was worth that bitch not answering just to hear Cristina's voice.

"Hi. You have reached the phone of the world's greatest mom. Please leave a message." *Beep*.

Even when she is talking about her banshee of a mother, I am forced to smile. Love that little girl.

I hung the phone up and just closed my eyes for a moment, then reached in the drawer where the pill bottle was and took them out. After popping one in my mouth, I put the bottle in my coat pocket. The way this day was going, I felt better knowing that they were near.

I looked at my computer screen and noticed it had finished loading. Having been around long enough I was able to maneuver my way around the web rather quickly. With just a few clicks I found what I was looking for in our database. When I need to protect the identity of someone, I simply delete a few items of evidence. Done it plenty of times. With the Feds involved, it is almost routine to delete shit. If they found out, things would be very, unnecessarily, messy. I figured that this person was not a prime suspect in the case anyway. Small potatoes.

AFTER I FINISHED AND SHUT DOWN MY COMPUTER, I WAS THIRSTY. I got up and went into the break area and poured another shit cup of coffee. With the smell of burnt beans and seeing as most of the dicks that work here have either gone home for the day or are out on a call, I think it would be safe to figure that this coffee has been brewing for a good hour or two.

THERE WAS HALF A BOX OF DUNKIN' DONUTS ON A SMALL TABLE next to the coffee. I opened it with hopes for a jelly or a glazed. No such luck. There was a chocolate that someone had cut in half and left the other half in the box. Who the fuck cuts a donut and eats half? Just eat it as much as you feel then throw the rest out! Do you really think by not eating the other half that your ass will be half as big?

"Doc," Bombshell Johnson was still here and stood in the doorway, "forensics is on line two."

Oh, shit!

I threw yet another coffee out (probably for the better) and quickstepped to my desk.

I picked up the phone and hit two. "George?"

"Hey, Doc. How are ya?"

"Just fucking peachy. What do you have for me?"

"Well, just as I figured, the blood and hair match a couple of the girls."

"No shit?"

"No shit."

"Did you find any prints? Any names?"

"Sure did." His quick response worried me. "Of course, the guy you nailed was an easy match. His prints are everywhere."

"Others?"

"Slow down pal. You have a bus to catch?" he joked. "Anywho, the other two that got away, I am faxing their info over to you now. They don't look like your average local yokels, if you know what I mean."

I had a feeling I knew what he meant.

"Good work, George. That it?"

"Well, yes and no. There were some faint prints on the cuffs. I ran them through the system, and I didn't get a match. Fubar, you know?"

"Nothing, huh?" I was relieved.

"Yeah, nothing. But it was coincidence that the Feds were here. They took a copy of the prints and said they would run it through their system up in Boston tomorrow morning. They said we should have something back by ten a.m."

The fucking Feds were there too? Shit!

"Hey, speaking of Feds, how's yours doing?" he laughed.

"George, I have to let you go. Thanks for your help."

"Sure, Doc. Anytime."

I THOUGHT ABOUT MY NEXT MOVE FOR A MOMENT. I KNEW I HAD to get to Rogers, but I thought I could stop by my apartment first. Maybe bring some damn flowers to Francine and hope to smooth things out a little. I decided to give Tiffany a call.

Using the perp phone, because I didn't want her number getting traced by the department, I dialed.

"Hello?"

"Hi, Tiffany. It's me, Jack."

"Oh, hi."

"How's our friend doing?"

"He's sleeping it off on my couch at the moment. He was pretty wild there for bit, paranoid and thinking my place was bugged. He was looking under every friggin thing. I had to give him an oxy."

"You gave him OxyContin? Tiffany!"

"Jack, it was all I had. And he was starting to freak me out."

"Holy shit! You just drugged a federal agent! How did you get him to take it?"

"Take it easy, Jack. It was only ten milligrams. I told him it was candy. He said he loved candy and mentioned something about a Jolly Rancher. I just wanted to slow him down a little. He's a fucking lightweight. Knocked him out."

"Alright, Tiffany, alright. Just keep an eye on

him. I'll be there in a few. I just have to make one stop first."

"Take your time, Jack. He's not freaking me out anymore. He's actually kind of cute, sleeping there."

Oh my god. "Okay, thank you. I'll see you in a little bit."

"Okay, bye, Jack."

I hung up and took an enormous breath. What the fuck?

I GOT UP TO LEAVE AND WAS ALMOST TO THE DOOR WHEN I REMEM-bered the fax George told me that he sent. I twisted on the spot and went to an area of the office that is crammed with shit: boxes full of print paper, envelopes, pens, and other shit you would find in an office. Our printer was huge, like the ones from the eighties. I don't know how it's still in operation. The fax machine spit the shit out one line at a time. *Buzz, buzz, buzz*. Luckily, it's a little out of the way so that when a fax comes through, we don't have to listen to it. If we did, it would have been thrown out of the window a long time ago.

The faxes were there. I noticed that one had fallen to the floor. After finishing, it usually spits the last piece of paper out, as if to say, "Here's your fax, you jerk!" It's like our own version of office road rage!

I looked at the pictures and I recognized the guys from a bust this past June. They were a bad bunch of apples. There was a lot of gunfire that ended up with four of them dead and one cop laid up in a bed at Rhode Island.

On my way to the door, I stopped by the chief's office.

"You wanted something, so here it is." I handed him the faxes. "These two got away this morning after I did in a third. I'm currently on the hunt for them. I have some ideas where they might be, but I'll keep you posted." Even though I knew very well where I might find them, I didn't want him to know.

"Alright, Jack, thanks. This will definitely hold them off for now. Why don't you get out of here? It's been a long day. You look like shit." He was doing his best at being a caring chief, but I've been here long enough. I know that he was just looking out for his own ass.

He was right about one thing: it had been a long fucking day and it's looking like it was going to be a long-ass night.

I headed for the exit.

CHAPTER SEVEN

I needed to get to Tiffany's, but I wanted to stop by my place first, but not until I stopped for a small bouquet from the plant department at Stop and Shop. Not the greatest looking bunch and a bit overpriced, but it'll have to do. Francine can be a bitch but when she is nice, she is *really* nice. Especially in the sex department, when my dick was working that is. She would be swinging from the chandelier, if we had one.

BY THE TIME I PULLED UP TO MY PLACE IN PAWTUCKET IT WAS nearing six. The five o'clock traffic on 95 is always a fucking mess.

I parked on the street then walked into my

apartment building. The sound of Spanish music and people talking was normal to hear from the other tenants; however, when I put my key in the hole, I realized that it wasn't even locked. I opened the door slowly. It was quiet.

Too quiet.

Unless she'd told me that she would be at her sister's, Francine was almost always here at this hour.

I placed the bouquet on the small stand by the door. With the shit of a day I had, there was little hesitation as I pulled out my gun. I kept to the quiet by gently closing the door behind me. I moved like a cat sneaking around looking for a mouse.

THE DAYLIGHT WAS FADING, SO THE PLACE WAS A LITTLE TOUGH to read. It reminded me of one night in Fallujah. We were getting ready to raid a home and as we were all standing outside, poised for entry, someone lit off a flare on the next street over. It was most likely an informant to the enemy letting them know that we were there. It lit us up like the noonday sun. We tried scattering like cockroaches, but we still took fire. Luckily, only a few wounded, no deaths. So, now, I know that if I turned on the lights, it might just give someone else the advantage. At least this way, the darkness would not only conceal him, but me as well.

With my gun raised up, I peered into the living room. Clear. I went left toward the bedroom. As I passed the bathroom, I gave a quick glance behind the shower curtain. Clear. I stepped into the bedroom. It was quiet and dark as usual. With my fucked-up sleep, I needed to be ready to lay down in a quiet, dark room at any time of day. Because of the broken bifold doors, the closet was always half open. Looking around I could see the room was empty. The only other room was the pantry. It was a sorry-ass example of a full kitchen, barely enough room in it for one person to maneuver, let alone hide someone. I made my way over to it while putting my gun back in the holster.

As I neared, I noticed a letter on the mini counter. I picked it up and unfolded it.

Jack,

You're a nice guy but I can't do this anymore. I can handle the sex shit, but the stress you're under is taking its toll on you. I see it in your eyes. Between your ex, your daughter, and work, I don't see much room left for me. Take care of yourself.

Francine
P.S. I left you a plate in the fridge. Hope you enjoy it.

I was a bit taken aback, but not surprised. I couldn't blame her considering the circumstances lately. Maybe after this case was over, I would give her a call. I opened the fridge and saw the plate of her latest concoction. It looked almost appetizing. I reached in to grab a beer behind it. It was definitely time for a drink. As I closed the door and turned around, I saw a face that surprised me.

"Hi, Jack."

MY HEAD HURT WHEN I WOKE UP ON MY PANTRY FLOOR. AS MY mind began to come back, I slowly lifted myself off the floor. My pants were wet, and I could smell beer. There was broken glass on the floor, so I guess I dropped the beer once I got knocked out. I made my way to the sink and wet a towel then stumbled a bit to the small table and chair. I put the cold towel on my head and tried to recall what had happened.

Impossible! Of any person to show up in my fucking pantry, Silva was the last one I thought I would see. I didn't understand the knock on the head either, but I would really like to repay him in kind, after I asked him some questions, of course.

I looked at the clock and saw that I had been out for about a half hour. I had to get to Tiffany's, so I cleaned myself up in the bathroom, took another pill, then left.

CHAPTER EIGHT

I arrived at Tiffany's about quarter after seven. After knocking, she answered the door and quickly put a finger on her lips as a sign for me to be quiet, then she invited me in.

I could see that Rogers was still out on the couch.

She motioned for me to come into the next room, so I followed her. It was her bedroom, but I knew it was just for conversing right now, not for what she used it for a few years ago. Not that I could even if she asked. As I entered, she closed the door behind me.

"What the hell happened?" she said as she lifted her gentle hand to my head.

"I had a visit from an old friend."

"Sit down. Let me clean it up." She went into the bathroom, and I heard a couple of cabinets open and close like she was looking for something. I sat down on the edge of the bed.

She came back in the room with some first aid stuff. My left arm was letting me know that I should probably have the dressing changed as well, so I unbuttoned my shirt.

"Jeez, Jack. How about dinner first?"

I looked up and gave her a little smile.

"I wouldn't mind taking you up on that sometime, but I was hoping that you could help me change these bandages," I asked her as I pointed to my arm.

"Holy shit, Jack. You should reconsider who you choose to be friends with."

AFTER SHE FINISHED, I STARTED PUTTING MY SHIRT BACK ON. "How's he doing?"

"Oh, he's still out," she said as she opened the door a little just as Rogers let out a snort.

"Are you hungry?" she asked concernedly.

"A little."

"I'll make you a sandwich. You like tuna?"

"That would be great."

As she went into the kitchen, I quietly went over to Rogers. I searched his pockets and took out his

ID. His picture didn't make him look any fucking better, the poor sap.

In the doorway to the kitchen, I told Tiffany that I had a couple things to do but it shouldn't take too long.

"No problem, Jack." She gave me the sandwich on a plate, cut in half corner-to-corner, with a pickle on the side. Then handed me a couple of pills.

"Just in case you get hit on the other side of your head."

I knew they were oxys.

I thanked her and took her generosity to go.

THE NIGHT AIR HADN'T GIVEN IN TO THE SUMMER-LIKE TEMPERAtures just yet, so I put the sandwich down on the passenger seat then put on the ragtop. After I drove down the street a bit, taking a bite of her sandwich, I muddled over my next move.

The fact that Silva was alive was evidence enough that some shit was going on, and it was obviously making its way through the system. He had to have help faking his death, but why? And why was he in my place? And why did he knock me on the head? Was Jimmy going to surprise me in the bathroom while I was taking a shit? I could only hope.

I should give his wife a call. See how she is.

I pulled over in front of E. P. Wieners on Taunton Ave. They were closed two o'clock on Mondays, and there was very little foot traffic around. I pulled out my cell phone as I took a bite of pickle.

As I dialed the number, I had an eerie feeling, like I was calling Jimmy. We used to do a lot of shit together. The department's softball team was where we really hit it off. Well, he hit me rather. He was playing second base when I decided to steal. The pitch was thrown, strike called, then the catcher threw it to Jimmy in hopes to get me out. He would have, so at the last minute I turned back toward first. Jimmy caught the ball and made a quick attempt to throw it to first but ended up hitting me in the back. We laughed about that for, well, up until he was killed.

Lucy's mother answered the phone with a soft, sullen tone.

"Hello?"

"Hi, Lauren, this is Jack." Given normal circumstances, Lauren was a funny character. She always had some wisecrack or joke about cops. Today, however, was not your normal circumstances day.

"Oh, hi Jack."

"I just wanted to call and see how, well..." Death always sucks, no matter how used to it you are. "Just to see if you guys needed anything."

"Oh, that's nice. I think we are all set right now

but I'm sure Lucy would love to hear your voice." With no brothers of her own, I was the next best thing. "Hang on. I'll get her."

A few seconds later I heard Lucy's voice.

"Hello?" She had the voice of someone who had been doing a lot of crying and could probably start again at any second.

"Hi, Lucy."

"Oh, Jack. Thank you for calling."

"No problem at all, Lucy. You hang in there, okay?"

"I'm doing my best, Jack." She started sobbing. "Tell me you know who did this, Jack! Tell me you are going to get them! Make them pay, Jack! Make them suffer!"

There was a pause, then Lauren got back on the phone.

"She's taking it kind of hard. The doctor gave her some Citalopram. I'm going to give her one now. Try and stop by sometime tomorrow if you can."

"I will Lauren. I will."

"Bye."

I THINK IT IS TIME TO PAY A VISIT TO MY TWO FAX MACHINE friends.

CHAPTER NINE

It was just past eight o'clock when I pulled into the station. With Rogers's ID in my pocket, I made it up to my desk without being questioned. Before I went to see my two friends, I had to get this done so I could get Rogers his ID back before he came out of his dope-coma.

I logged in and was forced to wait, just as before. This gave me an opportunity to look around the empty room.

I found a copy of the *Providence Journal* laying across Sanchez's desk. I recognized the picture of Jimmy on the front page. Those fucking reporters don't waste a second. There was a picture of me on the lower right, describing the case. "Keep Your Daughters Locked Inside!" the headline went. These fucking people are causing chaos.

I threw the paper in the trash where it belonged and went back to my desk. The damn archaic computer was finally ready for me.

With Rogers's ID I was able to access the FBI mainframe. Just as I did earlier with our system, I located the evidence link. I searched, but what I was looking for wasn't there. Which meant that they hadn't processed it yet. Damn. I have to try again later.

I shut the computer down and headed out. Taking the stairs meant that I could sneak out the side door. No beat cop to say, "Hey, Doc, working late?"

Fuck off.

As I pushed the side door open a flood of lights and voices hit me like it was New Year's friggin eve!

"Hey, Doc, can we ask you a few questions?"

"Jack, is this related to the case?"

What the fuck? They don't quit! They must have seen my car and waited for me to come out.

"Look, just give me a little time. I'm on the case."

I tried making it to my car through the crowd.

"How is your wife holding up?" a voice said.

My wife? What the hell does my ex-wife have to do with it?

I stopped flat and turned around just before I got to my car. "She is my ex-wife, and I'm sure she is doing just fine."

Then I turned and went to slide in my window like the Dukes of Hazzard.

"That doesn't sound like a concerned mother. Does she miss her daughter?"

Wait. What?

"What did you just say?" I started walking toward the scrawny, pinheaded dick with a big mouth.

The focus of attention was now on him and me.

His shaky voice muttered, "It's just that your daughter goes missing and you said your ex is fine with it."

All the shit that happened today suddenly traveled from my brain down to my fist as it squeezed closed.

Then, like a bullet, it shot into his face.

It happened so fast that it took us both by surprise.

If not for the few reporters behind him to fall into he would have been laid out on the pavement.

I got into my car, started it up, and with tires squealing, I left.

CHAPTER TEN

I didn't get too far down the street before I grabbed my phone and dialed Monica's number. It rang several times before someone answered.

"Hello?"

"Hello. Who is this?"

"My name is Doctor Simons. Who is this, please?"

"Jack," I said very simply. "Where is Monica?"

She must have understood that I was her ex-husband, but without compromising the HIPAA laws, she stated, "I think you should come down to the emergency room at Rhode Island Hospital."

Without another word, I hung up the phone and steered my already speeding car toward the hospital.

What the hell is going on? In the hospital?

There were so many questions racing through my mind, but my main concern was for Cristina.

I STOPPED WITH A SKID OUTSIDE THE EMERGENCY ROOM ONLY A few minutes after I spoke to the doctor. I jumped out and ran inside, busting through the small gathering of reporters that apparently had been informed of this situation from their leaky source, who usually gets paid a decent amount. Or so I'm told.

"Where is Monica Modene?" I asked the woman at the front desk.

While she scrolled through the computer looking for the name, I heard my name.

"Jack, over here."

I looked down the hall to Bobby, waddling his way toward me.

"Chief, what's going on?"

"I came down as soon as I heard. Monica's been hurt."

"By whom? And where is Cristina?"

He started leading me down toward the rooms in the emergency department.

"She only told us that it was two guys. They came in and took Cristina but not before working Monica over. You should go in and talk to her."

"How bad is she?" We stopped right outside the room where she was lying.

"Just talk to her," the chief replied.

I went in. The room was full of beeping, lights, and white coats talking to each other. They were around her tending to her wounds. I made it up to the head of the bed then leaned down to see a bloody, swollen face.

"Monica?"

No response.

"Hey, Monica?" I said again, softly.

Her left eye was swollen shut, but she started to open her right one.

"Jack?" she said in a very quiet and raspy voice.

"Monica, can you tell me what happened? Who did this?"

"They took our daughter, Jack!"

"Who did, Monica? Who?"

She didn't answer and her eye fell shut again.

I felt a hand on my shoulder. As I turned my head, a woman in a white coat said, "I'm Doctor Simons. Can we talk outside?"

I looked back at Monica for a moment then let the doctor lead the way.

Just outside the room she turned to me.

"She was beaten pretty badly."

NO SHIT!

"How bad?"

"Multiple fractures, some internal bleeding. We are going to take her up to surgery now."

Feeling almost helpless, I tipped my head down and put my right hand on my forehead. As much as I despised her, I didn't want Cristina growing up without a mother.

Cristina!

I lifted my head up. "Did she say anything about our daughter Cristina? Anything at all?"

"She talked a little to the detective." She motioned her head toward Bobby. "We have to move her now. Leave your number with the front and we will let you know how she is."

"Thanks, Doc." Felt a little weird saying it to someone else.

I've seen that look in a doctor's eyes before. Too many times. The look of desperation for a patient. The urgency to attempt the impossible.

AS I WATCHED THEM ROLL MONICA AWAY, THE THOUGHTS OF OUR very brief "good days" together circled inside my head.

Like the time we went to Rocky Point Park and ended up getting stuck on the Skyliner, which is a gondola suspended on a cable and was only ridden by lovers or people who jumped off at the top

to smoke weed. We were not the weed type. We enjoyed the pause as we overlooked the park and listened to Pearl Jam playing at the palladium. We seemed to be stuck up there forever, but we didn't care. We were in love. It was then that she told me that she was pregnant. I was so happy. We kissed, hugged, and even shed a few tears. It was a moment in my life that I would never forget.

I TURNED AND WALKED OVER TO WHERE BOBBY WAS SITTING (HIS normal stance).

"Here, Jack."

He handed me a cup of Dunkin' Donuts coffee. I

opened the lid and took a sip. Much better than the damn coffee at the station. Exhausted and feeling beaten myself, I sat next to him.

"What did she tell you, Bobby?"

"She couldn't talk too much but apparently there was two of them. She just kept saying that 'they took my baby.' They gave her some morphine. We have forensics at her place now."

Jesus Christ.

"She did say one thing, Jack."

My eyes perked up like he was about to give me what I needed to know.

"She said, 'Ask Jack. He knows where she is. He'll find her.' Do you know what she meant, Jack?"

My eyes went gloomy again.

"Is there something you're not telling me, Jack?"

With my head tilted toward the floor, I gave him a look out of the corner of my eye.

"Thanks for the coffee, Chief."

I stood up and walked to the woman at reception, gave her my number, then headed out the door.

The number of reporters was growing, but the news of what happened to the last reporter that stuck his nose in my face must have spread. There was only one comment as I got in my car.

"Go get 'em, Doc."

You bet your ass!

CHAPTER ELEVEN

Federal Hill, Providence, Rhode Island

According to Wikipedia, the 1870s saw the first arrival of immigrants from southern Italy, with greater numbers arriving in the next two decades. By 1895, the Hill was divided almost evenly between Irish and Italians. These were tension-filled times, as both groups fought for jobs and respect from the Yankee majority.

The first two decades of the 20th century witnessed heavy Italian-American immigration into Federal Hill, making it the city's informal Little Italy. Though the area today is more diverse, Federal Hill still retains its status as the traditional center for the city's Italian-American community.

In 1954, Raymond Loreda Salvatore Patriarca Sr, the newly appointed boss of the New England Faction of La Cosa Nostra (now known as the Patri-

arca Crime Family), made drastic changes to the family, the biggest being moving the family's base of operations from Boston to Atwells Ave in Federal Hill. He ran the crime family from 1954 until 1984 from the National Cigarette Service Company and Coin-O-Matic Distributors, a vending machine and pinball business on Atwells Avenue. The business was known to family members as "The Office."

The gateway arch over Atwells Avenue near downtown is one of the most recognizable landmarks in Providence. The La Pigna (or The Pine Cone) sculpture hanging from its center — a traditional Italian symbol of welcome, abundance, and quality — is often mistakenly referred to as "The Pineapple" and has become the symbol of Federal Hill.

Now, anyone that knows Federal Hill knows that you don't go up there to fuck around. If you have business, you attend to it, maybe have a nice meal, then you get the fuck out. That is, unless you happen to be connected, which means that you know someone who is someone. Me, I'm a nobody, and a cop, which gives me no good reason to go up there.

Tonight, though, I had to get to Camille's. One of the fanciest Italian eateries on the Hill with shit on the menu I can't afford on my salary, but eating was not the reason for my visit.

As I passed under the “pineapple,” I took a left down Bradford Street. Camille’s was just down on the right. As I drove up, I noticed that the greeter/bouncer/I-don’t-give-a-shit guy that usually hangs by the front door was not there. I stopped and looked at the hours sign: “Monday – Closed.”

Fucking wonderful.

I drove around the back and noticed a couple of cars parked near a door that was probably used by the kitchen and wait staff to sneak out and take a quick smoke break. The tiny light above the door was just bright enough to illuminate the fat face of the greeter I was expecting at the front door.

I pulled into the lot and parked my car next to one of the others. They were the kind of cars that you would expect to see on the Hill. One was a Lincoln Continental and the other, a Cadillac.

I shut off my engine, checked my gun for ammo (habit), and then jumped out of the window. The fat face got up off his chair as I walked over to him.

"Fuck you want, Jack."

I put my "I mean business" face on.

"I need to talk to Carmine."

"Then I suggest you go down to the corner and put a quarter in a phone and call him. He's not seeing anyone tonight. Not without an appointment."

Being a cop on the Hill didn't mean shit. I could have shown him my badge and he would, more than likely, try to stick it up my ass. Or, at least, tell me to do so.

"Look, Mike, this is urgent. Can you just go in and tell him that I am here?"

He folded his arms over his chest and didn't say a word. I obviously was not getting through to his peanut brain.

Mike was not a small guy. He had to weigh at least 280 pounds. Being tall and fat, I could barely see the door behind him.

What I would've liked to do was to just put a bullet in his head and walk over his corpse but reaching for my gun was probably what he was expecting. So, I did the next best thing.

I kicked him in the balls.

This massive load of shit in front of me unfolded his arms and, in a natural reaction, put both of his hands on his junk as he bent forward.

I then gave him a quick fist to his throat.

This rendered him useless as he fell forward. He was hurting. Alive, but still hurting, nonetheless.

I stepped over him as he lay there squealing in pain.

WITH GUN DRAWN, I OPENED THE DOOR. IT WAS A DARK HALLWAY, bathrooms on my right, and a lighted room further down on my left. The dining area, which I could see part of, was straight ahead. It was dark as well. I quietly started down the hall toward the light. As I got closer, I could hear voices, two to be exact.

I made it to just outside the room and was about to peek in when the men's bathroom door opened. I turned to see one of the two fax guys coming out. He suddenly saw me then pulled out his gun just as I ducked into the lighted kitchen.

"BOSS!"

I looked over to see Carmine and a "young" lady. Carmine was feeding her from a dish that he probably prepared to try to impress her, going by the cook's apron he was wearing. The girl let out a scream when she saw me.

I raised my gun to Carmine.

He lifted his hands as if I was placing him under arrest.

His crony from the bathroom came around the corner with his gun pointed at me and noticed mine was pointed at Carmine.

We all seemed to pause for a moment.

"What's going on, Carmine?" the girl asked.

With his arms still in the air and looking at me, "Shut up."

"I just want to talk, Carmine. Can we talk?" I pleaded.

Another pause.

"Let's all put the guns down. Nice and easy." Carmine was looking past me to the goon when he spoke.

I sensed that he was putting his gun down, so I lowered mine.

"Carmine, I thought you said we would be alone tonight."

Turning to his girl, he remarked "Hey, it friggin looks like something else came up, right?" He waved his arms in my general direction.

She had a look that only someone in the category of "not so bright, but good looks" would have. She gave a glance at me, then back at him.

"Yaa, I guess."

"Well, guess what? Here." He took some money

out of his pocket, like a father giving his daughter gas money. "This is for you. Get yourself somethin' nice and I'll see you Thursday. Have Mikey give you a ride home."

She was obviously less than pleased, but then he kissed her on the cheek to make her smile and help her forget about it. She turned and grabbed her purse and coat then blew him a kiss as she passed.

If you have ever had the "pleasure" of pissing off an Italian woman, then you know the look of death I was receiving the entire time she walked past me. I obviously ruined her date with "the Boss." She probably wished that they had shot me and threw me in the trunk of the caddy so that they could continue.

Carmine took off his apron and started cleaning his hands in the sink while his muscle still stood in the doorway.

"Well, Jack, a call would have sufficed. I must tell you, I'm not pleased. She's a nice girl."

I stepped closer. "I apologize, Carmine, but this is urgent."

Just then, Carmine's girl came rushing back in. "Carmine! Mikey's hurt!"

Carmine paused then glanced at me for a moment. He shook his head in a disapproving way, then gave a wave to his guy as if to tell him to go clean it up.

His muscle didn't leave right away. He looked at me then back at Carmine.

"I'll be okay. Jack's not going to touch me. Are you, Jack?"

"No." Unless he gave me a good fucking reason to. So far, I am not too sure.

Carmine's girl and the goon left.

"Well, Jack, now you have me all to yourself," he said as he dried his hands on a towel. "Now, what the fuck do you want?!" His demeanor changed dramatically.

Even though I was a detective with a gun under my arm, I was shitting my pants.

CHAPTER TWELVE

Carmine finished cleaning up and we moved to the dining area and sat at a table. That is, I sat at a table; Carmine sat up against the mirrored wall, in a comfy, Italian booth. I sat across from him in a chair that, I'm pretty sure, was made for a kid. He sat there with his arms resting on the tops of the cushioned back. The mirror would probably be great in the daytime with the light coming in through the windows. I could only imagine some heavy coming in to kill an unsuspecting rat but getting seen in the mirror and shot first. However, in this light it was useless. The only light in the room came from the kitchen and it was just enough for us to see each other, nothing more. He could reach under the table and pull out a fucking shotgun and I wouldn't see it coming.

I started, "I would have called first, but after our conversation this morning I needed to talk to you in person."

"Yeah, this morning was a little rough. One of my best guys got whacked. You know anything about that, Jack?" His staring eyes glowed in the darkness.

"I'm not sure, maybe I could ask my partner what he saw. Oh, wait, no, he's dead."

"Oh, Jimmy. I liked him. He was a good boy. A little too naive though. Not a place for guys like him, this business."

Just the fact that he was comparing his thug to Jimmy was pissing me off. I thought I'd better get to it, the business.

"We had a deal, Carmine. I gave you information, whatever you needed, and you kept my daughter safe."

"And?"

"And?" I leaned forward and banged my fist on the table. "My daughter is missing! And her mother is in critical condition at Rhode Island Hospital!"

"Jack, try to control yourself. We wouldn't want anything getting," he pulled his arm down slowly and from the top of the cushion I could see that he had grabbed a gun, which he was now holding on the table and pointing it at me, "*blown* out of proportion."

I was forced to remember my place, here on the Hill, so I sat back in my *mini* chair.

"I apologize, Carmine. It's just, it's my daughter."

"Did I say that your daughter wasn't safe, Jack? Huh?"

A glimmer of light in this dark-ass room.

"No. No, I guess you didn't." I felt a certain amount of relief. "So, she's, okay?"

"Of course, well, for the time being."

"Wait! What do you mean?"

Just then a shadow appeared in the darkness of the mirror behind Carmine, still too dark to make out a face, but no matter. I knew who it was without having to turn around.

He raised his right hand, which was holding something that I had a feeling was not a goddamn Build-A-Bear. Before I had a chance to pull out my gun, I saw stars and then nothing.

WHEN I CAME TO, I WAS TIED TO THE SAME DUMBASS CHAIR. ALL these big ass Italian guys and I get tied to fucking Tiny Tim's chair!

I tasted blood on my right cheek that was obviously coming from yet another gash on my head. I was hunched forward, and drool was dripping out of my mouth. Without looking up I knew who was there.

"Well, Silva, at least you hit me on the opposite side of my head this time."

"Sorry, Jack. I just grabbed the first thing I could find when I came in. A fucking rolling pin! Can you believe it? I feel like my mother holding it!" He laughed with his own amusement, waving it towards Carmine.

Carmine started to laugh.

"Hilarious." I couldn't hold back my sarcasm.

"Looks like it really hurts too," Silva noted as he poked at the gash.

I jerked away. "Why don't you untie me so I can let you know how it feels?"

"Oh, sorry Jack. No can do."

The laughter subsided.

"When I ran into Silva earlier," I said to Carmine, "I had a feeling that you guys might be working together."

"Working together?" Carmine started a new round of laughter. "No offense to you two shmucks but I don't work with cops." He walked over to the bar and proceeded to open a bottle of wine.

"Then you must be working for him." I motioned to Silva, as if he could be the boss of anything.

"Oh, Jack, Jack, Jack." Carmine poured himself

a glass of wine. "I work for one thing, and one thing only."

"Don't tell me it's for the money. Because that is just tacky."

"Jack, you think I can live off what this restaurant pulls in?"

"Well, the fucking prices are outrageous," I couldn't help mentioning.

"True, but people don't complain. Unlike yourself, they know better, and they tend to make more than the usual Providence PD salary. No offense." He motioned to Silva.

Silva simply raised his hands in a "no offense taken" kind of way.

"But you gave me your word. I thought that meant something up here on the Hill."

"Of course, it does. If I was talking to another goombah. To a cop, you're lucky I even let you in here. And the fact that you diddlers seem to be having a problem and involving my place of business is beginning to upset me!"

"Hey, I'm not a diddler!" Silva exclaimed.

"Honestly, I don't care anymore what you are. I assume you came here to give my final payment?"

"That I did," Silva replied.

Silva picked up a blue gym bag from the shadows behind him and put it on the table in front of me. Carmine put his wine down and unzipped the bag. He reached in and pulled out a couple of stacks of what looked like hundred-dollar bills.

"It's all there," Silva assured.

Carmine put the money back in and zipped it shut.

"Good. Then we are done here."

There was a small pause, then Silva pointed to me.

"What about him?"

"He's not my problem. He's yours. And I suggest you deal with it."

Silva thought for a moment then asked, "Hey, don't you have connections at the Johnston landfill?"

"I do, dipshit, but they are MY connections, not yours."

"Oh, okay." Silva pulled out a gun from behind his back and aimed it at my head.

"Whoa! What the fuck are you doing?"

"What? You told me to deal with it."

"Not in my place of business, asshole."

"Oh, sorry. You are right." Silva put his gun behind his back again.

"Look, you have the girl, right?" Carmine implied.

"Yeah."

"Well, this is the girl's FATHER. Capeesh?"

It took Silva a second to figure it out, but it hit him. "Yeeeaaahhh. That's right!"

"Oh, for shit's sake. What the fuck would you cops do without me?"

Neither I nor Silva gave a response. Carmine picked up his glass again.

"Look, just wait till my boy gets back. He'll help you get him in the trunk."

"Trunk?" I let out a gasp. Not very fond of closed-in places.

Carmine gave a look to Silva and then back to me.

Then the lights went out again.

CHAPTER THIRTEEN

"Hello. Are you there?" Tiffany was shaking Rogers's left shoulder, hoping to revive him.

"Huh?"

"How are you feeling?"

"I, um, I'm not sure."

Rogers was coming out of his medicinally induced coma. Trying to sit upright on Tiffany's wonderfully comfortable couch.

"Where am I? Who are you?"

"My name is Tiffany. I'm a friend of Jacks. You remember Jack?"

"Yeah, sure, I think so. But how did I get here?"

"Well, it's kind of a long story. But you're safe here."

"Safe? From what?" Rogers began rubbing his eyes.

"Well, Jack had some stuff to take care of and he didn't want you to get hurt, I suppose."

"Hurt? That just doesn't make sense."

"Well, you would understand if you would have seen what kind of shape he was in when he brought you here, but you were in pretty messed up shape as well."

"What time is it?"

"It's just about nine thirty."

"PM?"

"That's right. Why don't I fix you some tea?" Tiffany stood up and headed to the kitchen.

Rogers was rubbing his temples and trying to remember anything that happened. *The last thing I remember was being at the crime scene, then taking a ride*, he thought to himself.

Tiffany reentered the room with a cup, steam floating from the top. "Luckily, I already had the water on. I was hoping Jack would be here by now."

"How long has he been gone?" Rogers took the cup and held it with both hands.

"I don't know. Over an hour. But when he left, he said he wouldn't be long. To tell you the truth I am starting to get worried."

"Did you try his cell?"

"I did, but no answer."

Rogers sipped his hot tea, then placed it on the coffee table. With the thought of Jack not answering his cell phone he decided to try his own phone. He put his hand in his coat pocket but couldn't find it.

"Do you know where my phone is?" he said as he started feeling each of his pockets as if he was pretending that he didn't have any money when being approached by a homeless beggar.

"Oh, I took it out and put it in my bedroom. It kept ringing and I didn't want it to wake you. I'll go get it."

While she did that, Rogers took another sip of his tea.

"This tea is delicious. What kind is it?" he asked when she came back.

"Just plain ole Lipton with a dash of honey." She smiled then handed him his phone.

"Thank you."

"You're welcome."

"I mean, for the tea."

"You're welcome for that too." Her smile grew bigger.

Rogers put the tea down and began looking through his phone.

"Shit."

"What's shit?"

"The office has been calling. A few times. I have to call them back."

As Rogers dialed, Tiffany went back into the kitchen. A few moments later she came out with some tuna fish sandwiches with pickle spears on the side, put them down on the table, then sat down next to him.

Talking into his phone, Rogers protested "I understand. I was on a case and couldn't be reached." Rogers thought he had to lie even though it was kind of true. He was out of reach.

There was a pause in the room.

"I did what?"

"Well, I had to follow up on some evidence. Listen, I will call you tomorrow and give you a full report. Okay?"

Another pause, then he said good-bye.

The look on his face after he hung up was concerning to Tiffany.

"What did they say?"

"Said that he got a call from the IS department that I logged into our system with an outside computer and accessed the evidence from this case. That kind of stuff throws up a red flag. But how could someone log into our system as me when I was here asleep?"

Tiffany had a puzzled look as if to say, "I have no idea."

Rogers started going through his pockets again. This time he found his wallet and quickly pulled it out. When he opened it, right away he had his answer.

CHAPTER FOURTEEN

When the lights started coming on again, it was a slow process. Like the Showcase theater turning the house lights on very slowly after a bad movie. And to think, I wasn't even offered popcorn.

I also realized that I wasn't tied to the mini chair anymore. Instead, I was cuffed to a pipe in the ceiling.

The ride in the trunk that got me here must have been full of pine needles from this past Christmas, because I had them stuck all over me.

More drool was coming from my mouth, and I could taste even more blood from yet another hit to my head. If I get out of this situation, I am going to hit Silva in his fucking head so many times he will think he was a piñata.

I was hanging there for so long that my arms had gotten tingly then went numb from gravity forcing the blood to my lower extremities. The good thing is that I couldn't feel much of the pain from the bullet wound on my arm anymore.

There was hardly a light on, but I had the feeling that I was in a basement. The musty, damp smell, the dirt floor; it was definitely not of new construction.

I could hear rain and thunder which immediately forced me to wonder if I had put the ragtop on, but the details of this day were becoming fuzzy, and I couldn't quite remember. Another blow to the head would probably erase my mind altogether.

WHAT SEEMED LIKE AN ETERNITY PASSED BEFORE I HEARD A DOOR open, then close. No footsteps were the advantage of a dirt floor, but I sensed someone was getting closer. With me in this vulnerable state, I considered the idea that it could be my killer. That my final moments on this earth could be near. A feeling that I had felt many times before.

A shadow entered the doorway.

"Hi, Jack."

Fucking Silva. Who else could it be?

"Fuck you want, Silva?"

"Hey, take it easy. Why are you so pissed?"

"Oh, I don't know. Maybe the fact that you busted my head a few times today? Or you came back from the dead for the sole purpose of kidnapping kids and killing them?"

"Jack, you are not seeing the big picture here."

"Where's my daughter?"

"She's in the middle of something right now."

"WHERE'S MY DAUGHTER, YOU SICK FUCK? I swear if you touch one single hair—"

"Jack," Silva spoke as he walked in a slow circle around me. Stopping behind me, he came closer to my ear and spoke softly. "Your daughter is the answer. The answer to a riddle I have been trying to solve for a long time."

"Let me see her. Please." Me, begging; I was finally succumbing to this predicament.

"No can do right now, Jack. But when they are finished, I will let her come in and say good-bye."

I glared up from the dirt floor.

"What do you mean, good-bye?"

At that moment there was another opening and closing of the door.

"Well, who could that be?" Silva played as he pulled out his gun and moved into the shadows along the wall.

The person stepped into the doorway, just as had Silva, and stood there for a moment. The ominous darkness of night gave the silhouette a hooded appearance. The arms raised up in a synchronous motion and, together, they pushed the hood backward.

A flash of lightning was enough to illuminate the appearance.

"Jack?"

"Francine? What the hell are you doing here?"

"Yes, Francine, what *are* you doing here?" Silva revealed his position from the shadows.

"Watch it! He has a gun!"

Silva's gun seemed to catch just enough light to be intimidating as he held it straight outward from his hip.

"Oh my. Whatever should I do? Are you going to kill me?" she asked as Silva walked slowly closer.

She raised her hands in the air.

"Silva, she has nothing to do with this! Leave her out of it!"

Silva walked right up to her. Francine lowered her hands and put them behind her back.

"I think you like it better this way. Don't you?"

Silva lowered his gun and put his left arm around Francine's midsection, pulled her close, then gave her a ravenous kiss.

She gave no resistance.

If light were emitted out of my eyes, with as wide as they were now, they would've easily lit up this dreary room. My mouth still had a bit of drool and blood dripping out, but its fall to the floor from my lower lip had just gotten that much closer.

“Francine,” I broke this nasty silence, “what the fuck are you doing?”

The couple that had been sharing an erotic embrace right in front of me finally broke apart.

“Oh, hi, Jack. Forgot you were here for a moment.”

CHAPTER FIFTEEN

"What's going on? I feel...strange."

Rogers was still on the couch where Tiffany had left him. His arms felt heavy, his mind was blank, and the only thing he could see was the tea and tuna sandwich on the table.

Feeling nauseous, he tried to get up in search of a bathroom, because, he thought, it would not be pleasant to vomit on someone's living room carpet. He moved to the edge of the couch and gave a slight push to raise himself but was quickly unfulfilled as he fell, as if every cell in his body were cement, onto the carpet.

With his face pressed against the floor, he began to vomit, then passed out cold. There he stayed, incontestably motionless.

CHAPTER SIXTEEN

"So, let me get this straight, you two have been seeing each other without telling me? Why am I not surprised?"

"That's right, Jack. Remember when I 'died'?"

"Vaguely," I said sarcastically.

"Well, I needed to make some drastic changes to my life."

"Drastic? That's an understatement." I continued with my unimpressed tone, "What about your wife? How does she fit into this?"

"Well," Silva was a little hesitant to give me any information, but with me being bound and more than likely not going to survive the night, he figured he would entertain my questioning. "When she found out she was not at all understanding.

Especially knowing Francine was pregnant with my child."

My expression could not get any more shocked. My head is fucking spinning. Speechless.

"She, of course, wanted a divorce. However, with her being in a new position with the city council and me being a cop, the papers would eat us for breakfast."

"Oh, let's just get this over with. All this talk about your wife is upsetting me." Francine was less than sympathetic.

"All in good time, my dear. Jack is not going anywhere. And besides, he might as well know why we are going to kill him."

"Oh, all right."

"Wait, you guys have a kid?"

"Yes, Jack," Francine said as she began to move slowly closer to me. "Remember when I told you I was going to Florida to take care of a sick aunt?"

"Yeah, kind of." It was a few years back. Apparently, about eight friggin years ago.

"Well, I 'kind of' had a baby during that time. Silva has a cousin that I stayed with. She was quite nice." She smiled and looked at Silva.

"And while she was gone," Silva interjected, "I had a nice talk with my wife. We both agreed to stay married for the public eye. However, because we have been doing a lot of research and testing, which both require a bit of cash, the funds were running low. We all were getting a little edgy, so I designed a way to increase our cash flow and take the public eye away from her at the same time."

"So, you faked your own death."

"That's right, Jack."

"But the body in the Blackstone? The medical records?"

"You think I was at Carmine's getting a fucking cannoli, Jack?" He gave a small laugh with a spurt of air through his lips.

"There are plenty of Silvas out there, and with a little doctoring of the records, I was as good as dead. That took care of the public eye, and thanks to the friendly neighborhood policeman's death or dismemberment policy, my wife was able to collect very handsomely."

"Where is Rogers, Francine?" My arms were very uncomfortable, but I continued to ask questions. I figured if I kept stalling that maybe they would forget about killing me. Doubtful.

"Rogers? Who the hell is Rogers?" Francine questioned.

"Oh, yes, how is our Fed doing?" Silva inquired.

"Fed?! You mean to tell me that the Feds are in this now?"

"Take it easy, Francine. I bet Jack dropped him off at Tiffany's. Didn't you, Jack?"

Silva sounded very smug, but he had every right to. How the hell would he even know this? I tried not to look surprised, but he saw right through my poker face.

"Oh, that's right, Jack. Carmine has been quite valuable. He had one of his men follow you after Jimmy was killed. We both figured you needed to be kept an eye on."

"You are a piece of work. How did you manage to hypnotize these people with your craziness?" I interjected.

He turned and gave me a very angry stare, like I had just poked the damn bear. I could see that this was going south real fucking fast.

I quickly continued with some questions to take his mind off Francine. She may be a whacked-out, crazy bitch, but she was the only angle I had at the moment.

"I don't understand. What testing?"

There was a brief, uncomfortable pause. Then Silva turned back to Francine. "Why don't you go get her? I think it's time she finally met Uncle Jack."

"If you wish." Francine pattered away in silence. She seemed to be growing tired of this situation. Probably after hearing that the Feds were involved.

CHAPTER SEVENTEEN

The storm outside was getting heavier. The thunder and lightning were increasing as if it were indicative of the storm that was underway in this musty place. I enjoyed the flashes of light as they chased away the darkness, but they were reminiscent of the fight we were engaged in while in Iraq.

We were just two clicks outside of the city when we were greeted by heavy fire. One of my men was dead and another wounded badly. I called in air support as we found shelter behind a charcoal-toasted truck that was probably used by an unsuccessful car bomber. It was dark, somewhere in the middle of the night, but with the rockets going in and out of the city, it was lit up as if it was fucking high noon. It was, as this one, just another shit situation.

I made it out of the Middle East alive, and with any luck, I hoped to do the same here.

"JACK."

My attention was drawn back to Silva.

"You look like shit."

I gave a half smile. "Whatever you are up to," I was poking again, "I hope that it's worth it."

He came closer, too close. He didn't have to; I could smell his shit from across the room. Like on trash day in the summer heat; as soon as you heard the dump truck on the street over, you could smell the rot that was hidden inside it. It was a sense reflex, like you couldn't know one without the other.

"Jack," he spoke softly but I could feel his breath on my face, "you would do anything for your daughter, *right*?"

"Yes, but..."

"ANNNYTHINNG?" His crazy was starting to ooze out of his friggin ears.

"Anything."

"Would you *die* for her?"

His eyes were wide open, and they reminded me of Igor in *Young Frankenstein*. I felt I had to choose my next words very carefully.

The only phrase that came to mind was from

my favorite actor, Humphry Bogart: "There's no sacrifice too great for a chance at immortality." Oh shit! Why did I just say that?

"Very poetic, but you are goddamn right on that one, Jack!" He started to back away, thankfully. Asshat.

"There isn't a single thing that I wouldn't do for *my* daughter," he continued. "Since the day she was born I have been under her control. Mystified by her. 'Did she have enough to eat?' 'Is she warm enough?' 'Is she cool enough?' 'Am I giving her enough love?'"

Poor sap was in a monologue, which gave me time to peek up at my shackles. If I pulled hard on the pipe I was connected to, considering the dampness and age of the upper wood floor beam that the pipe was fastened to, it might just pull the nails out and I could slide off the end of the pipe. It had nothing but a cap on it, which, with my laymen's education of randomness, gave me the notion that it might be a gas pipe. I just hoped it wouldn't crack with my doing so and blow us all to hell.

"Well, Jack, this is no different. She *deserves* to have everything she wants. If she wants something I don't have, then I will find a way to give it to her. Even if it means that I must sacrifice myself for it."

He obviously had some daddy issues going on in

his fucking head. But this was not a good time for me to get all Sigmund Freud on his ass.

JUST THEN THERE WAS A FLASH OF LIGHT, AND THE LIGHTS WENT out. We were both taken by surprise. I started pulling hard on the pipe with what energy I had left. I could feel it starting to come free.

There was another flash of light and for a moment the room was illuminated. A split second was long enough for us both to lock our eyes on each other. What I saw was his position closer to me. Obviously, he had been searching for me in the darkness. What he saw was my feet pressed against the ceiling, upside-down and pulling on the pipe.

When the lightning had flashed, I paused my pulling, knowing that he would try to stop me, so I dropped my legs and in the cover of darkness, I volleyed my foot, as hard as I could, in the direction I thought his face would be.

Well, his reaction was just as I had figured; he was advancing on me. My right foot did not make contact with his head, like I had hoped. It ended up being my knee to someplace on his left side. I heard him grunt a little with the hit, but he didn't slow as much as I had hoped. In the next instant he threw a blind punch. Damn ass lucky one, too.

He was just about to connect to my jaw when there was another flash of light. It gave his face a most gruesome look. The shadowing around his eyes and cheeks made him look old and worn out. Every pain that life had inflicted upon him was suddenly superimposed for the world to see.

After the hit to the jaw, I soon felt a sharp pain in the left side of my ribcage to match. Knocking the wind out of me. It became hard to breathe.

There was another light but this one wasn't a flash.

"Are you two about done?"

Francine had stepped into the doorway with just enough time to catch the punch to my ribs. She was holding a flashlight that gave off much more light than the single bulb that had been trying to illuminate this dungeon.

After my senses trickled back, I noticed that Francine was not alone. She was holding the hand of a little girl, about my daughter's height.

"Mommy, I don't wanna."

Francine turned. "It's okay dear. No one is going to hurt you. I want you to meet an old friend of mine. His name is Jack. Jack, this is Amy."

As they both took two steps closer, I was able to see Amy more clearly. But what I saw was not a beautiful little eight-year-old in the prime of her fun years. Her face was scarred, slightly disfigured. I could feel my forehead crouching down toward my eyes as I began to squint to see more detail of this hideous creature.

“Hello, Jack. Pleased to meet you,” she said with the voice of an angel.

“Uh, oh, hello to you, Amy.” My hesitation was an obvious reaction to my shock.

I turned to Silva. “What the hell have you done?”

Just as I thought that I could withstand any more beatings, Francine had swung her left arm up like a player for the Red Sox hitting one over the Green Monster. The palm of her hand connected with my right cheek so hard that I saw a few stars and then the sensation of needles started warming. I was positive that a third-degree burn would be more enjoyable.

“YOU WILL NOT CUSS IN FRONT OF AMY!” she growled murderously.

CHAPTER EIGHTEEN

G*ET UP!*

I SAID, GET UP, DAMN YOU!

The RPG hit was close. Close enough to take out two of my men and knock me down. My ears were ringing. Couldn't hear a fucking thing. All I remember was Gonzalez tugging on my vest.

GET THE FUCK UP! WE HAVE TO MOVE!

I stumbled to my feet and Gonzalez held onto my Kevlar vest tight as we ran for better cover.

Diving behind a wall and out of sight of imminent danger, he let me go and I was able to sit down and get myself in check. It took a good twenty minutes before I was able to hear anything besides the ringing.

To this day that ringing has subsided some, but it remains. Unless thwarted by some other noise, it rings like a phone in the distance. Always ringing. Never answered.

Francine's slap brought it back to the forefront.

ONCE I CAME BACK TO MYSELF, I GAVE THE MOST SERIOUS OF looks to Francine.

"I can take all the shit that this guy delivers, but from you, Francine, I fear our relationship may be in jeopardy."

She took a step forward and was winding up for another *monster* hit when Silva caught her arm in mid-swing.

"That's enough of that, for now." Silva gave her a cool smile and then nodded a little toward the door. Francine handed him the flashlight and gave a quick kiss.

Francine looked down at Amy. "Okay, let's go get some ice cream from the fridge."

"Yea!! Bye, Jack. It was nice to meet you." She spoke over her shoulder at me as they took hands and trotted off.

"Nice to meet you too, Amy," I called after her as they turned the corner then out of sight.

I hung there, exhausted. Dripping sweat and blood. I had nothing left. No second wind. No reinforcements were coming. I'd been beaten.

I looked at Silva.

He was looking at me with his crazy eyes again.

"If you are going to kill me and throw me in the river, just do it already."

"All in good time, Jack. But first, a drink."

"I don't need a drink." Even though I could use one, I didn't want one from him.

"Ah, but you do. You don't think you do, but you do."

I don't know if I'd just been hit in the head too much, but his crazy was starting to amuse me.

Silva took a bottle out of a black bag I hadn't noticed before now that was sitting against the wall. I watched him pour something into a glass about the size of a shot. Then he walked over to me.

"What are we toasting? And where's yours?"

"We are toasting to your liberation. But not of your mind, my friend. The liberation of your blood. An exodus, if you will."

"My blood? I kind of need that."

"Ah, but I need it more. You've seen that girl and how life has failed her. Gave her a losing hand. Well, with your help, I will deal her a hand of aces."

"Are you telling me that you didn't do that to her face?" I couldn't resist the sarcasm.

"Of course not, you sick fuck! That there is a medical anomaly. The rarest of diseases. It's called

Urbach-Wiethe disease. Do you know how many people have it, Jack?"

"One?" He didn't seem amused.

"Only about four hundred people have been diagnosed with it in the past ninety fucking years. We have been doing everything we can to try and give her a normal life, but people can be so damn cruel!" He raised an angry fist in the air.

Silva seemed to have forgotten about the shot glass in his hand, although I was curious what it was. I was awfully thirsty. But I'd better hold off on reminding him just to be safe.

"So why have these innocent young girls been getting pulled from the Blackstone without a face?"

Silva seemed excited to tell me. Like he had been wanting to get this off his chest for a long time but hadn't had the opportunity of having a *captive* audience.

"Jack, think my boy. If I could find a receptive donor, one that Amy's body would not reject, then she could have a normal face, and everyone would stop *STARING* at her!" Silva stared off into the darkness as if there were someone there that he was talking to. "I HAD to cut her face. Just a little. I had to see if it would take. The skin grafts. But Francine's medical experience is still lacking. She would cry after. Really cry. I told her that we had to. Try to be strong. You are a good girl. I love you."

He paused.

I didn't want to, but I had to bring him back. The silence was getting a little creepy, even for him.

"Couldn't you just ask a medical professional or, possibly, a donor bank?"

Silva turned and stared at me as if I had just lit a fuse under his ass.

"Don't you think I did that, Jack? Do you think I'm a fucking idiot?"

He moved to within an inch of my nose and stared me in the eyes.

"No?"

"BINGO, Jack. Bing-fucking-O," he snarled. "We've been to Mass. General, Hasbro, and even the goddamned Shriners. I checked, over and over again," he whispered frustratedly, "and there were some potential donors, but you know what? They were still alive, and after talking to some of the parents, they didn't want to *get involved.*"

He started to back away.

"People only care about their own kids. Assholes," he muttered through his teeth with a sound of hatred. "And besides," he continued, "people were starting to ask questions. It was starting to get attention from the wrong people. The press. That fat-ass chief of ours. He doesn't know shit!"

I couldn't disagree with him on that.

"So, why my daughter? Why me? We are not on any donor bank," I asked.

"That is correct. That is why I had to enlist the knowledge of Carmine and his friends. They have ways of finding information that is, let's say, not so common knowledge. When I showed up at your place earlier today, I was looking for your hair on a brush so I could check your DNA. Then you showed up and I thought 'why not just whack you and take some blood to make sure.' And it just so happened that you, yourself, asked for Carmine's help as well. I mean, what are the fucking chances? The very guy that was supposed to be keeping your daughter from me, was playing both sides. We were able to test your blood and, low and behold, you did contain the necessary gene as well as your daughter. Now we will have more than enough blood to, hopefully, finish what we started."

"You're mad. And I guess the man with the most money won this time."

"Exactly right, Jack. On both counts."

"Well, maybe I should have faked my death as well." I was getting sarcastic, not to his liking.

His full attention turned back to me.

"There will be no faking for you, Jack. Once you drink this you will become paralyzed. Not able to move a fucking muscle. It is a combination of pufferfish venom called tetrodotoxin mixed with a deliriant known as Datura. The Haitian voodoo doctors use it to turn people into zombies."

"So, you are making me into a zombie?" I toyed with him.

"Once you are in this state," he crept closer, "Jack, I will be able to do whatever damn thing I want to you, and you won't even be able to so much as blink your fucking eye."

CHAPTER NINETEEN

"Daddy, why are you and Mommy getting divorced? Did I do something wrong?" Cristina questioned me.

"Oh, no, no, no. Don't you ever think that, okay?" I knelt on one knee to be face to face with her. "It's just that sometimes mommies and daddies don't get along anymore. Their lives have just gone in two different directions, and they just can't find their way back."

"What will happen to me?"

"You, little one, will have the best life ever! We both love you so very much and that will never change. Okay?"

"Okay."

"How about you and I go to Sundaes for some ice cream?"

"YOU SAID I WOULD BE ABLE TO SEE MY DAUGHTER." HE COULD hear my desperation. I didn't care. I just wanted to see Cristina.

"Oh, that I did. Hmmm. Well, I suppose, what will it hurt. For old times' sake, eh?" Silva wanted to be a man of his word, even though his word didn't mean shit.

"For old times," I responded with a half-breath.

He placed the shot glass down near the bag and walked out of the room. A door opened then closed. I was alone. Wherever this was. He took the flashlight with him, so I was left with the darkness. The flashes of lightning had passed with the storm outside. All that was left was some light rain. I hung there like a slab of cow in a freezer. I was too tired to attempt another push off the ceiling. I chose to just wait. Wait for the inevitable.

CHAPTER TWENTY

When the phone rang George was not in any condition to move swiftly from his position. He had taken to his usual nightly location in front of the television watching reruns of *Law and Order*. He had seen most of them, but he liked watching them over again to see if there was a clue that he had missed the first time.

On his left was a folding table that was askew with a Pringles container, Jolly Rancher wrappers, and a Pepsi. His right hand was always touching the remote for the TV, so he was ready to turn the channel during unwanted commercials.

The phone rang again. George gave a sigh of discontent. He had been meaning to move the phone to his right-side table, but he has yet to get the gumption to do so.

A third ring. Considering that the phone might not stop, he gave in and stood up from his relaxed position. With eyes never leaving the screen, he walked over to the phone and picked it up.

"Hello?"

"George Coffee?"

"This is he."

"Hi, this is Agent DeMello up in Boston. We ran those prints for you."

"No, shit. Great. What ja' find out?"

"I'm faxing it to your office now. You should have a look."

"But I'm not at my office!" For Christ's sake.

"And after reviewing the file we have noticed some tampering."

"What do you mean, tampering?"

"As far as we can tell, someone got into our database. But nothing seems out of the ordinary, so far."

"Well, Mr. Boston, is that all you got?"

"Agent DeMello, and no. We've been trying to reach an agent of ours that has been attached to this case. Do you have any idea of his whereabouts?"

"You mean, Rogers?"

"Yes, that's him."

"I met him earlier today. I can poke the bushes around here and see what flies out."

"Okay, if you find him, have him give us a call."

"No problem."

After George hung up the phone, he realized that he missed a significant plot twist that Agent Benson had discovered.

"Damn, Olivia. I have to go." He blew her a kiss then shut the TV off before leaving.

CHAPTER TWENTY-ONE

"Your name is Captain Jack Daniels, correct?" The voice spoke out of the darkness. It was broken English, at best.

"Kiss my ass."

Another blow to the head.

"Wake up!" The voice came again. "Wake up, you stupid American scum!" Echoed with a splash of water.

My eyes crept open. There was some talk between two or three of them. It was hard to determine exactly.

"You will tell us the exact location and number of men that are with you, and the location of your base, or your eyes will be pulled from you head!"

"Go fuck yourself."

A fist came out of the darkness to my left, then I was out. Again.

"WAKE UP!"

"I said, wake up!"

I must have passed out. Listening to crazy tends to do that to me. Silva slapped me a few times to bring me back. Standing behind him was my beautiful Cristina. My eyes widened and I felt my heart beating stronger.

"Cristina!"

"Daddy!" she exclaimed as she ran and put her arms around me.

I wished that I could reach down and pick her up. Hold her. All I could do was tilt my head in her direction.

"Very touching," Silva mocked as he clapped at a slow interval.

"C'mon, Silva. It doesn't have to be like this. We can get your daughter some help. Just leave Cristina alone!" I pleaded with him.

He reached for her right arm to pull her away. He was able to unlock her grasp, but she then screamed and jerked her arm back around my waist.

"No! I want my daddy!"

He reached in and grabbed both her arms with force. "Let go!"

With his bent over position, as he pulled her away, I had an opportunity. I took it. I threw my left knee up with such force that when I hit his nose his head flew back, and then he was laid out on the floor.

Cristina came back to me again. Tighter this time. I hoped she would never let go.

Silva lay motionless for a few moments before he came to. He groaned a little then rolled himself over to his knees. With his right hand he felt the blood dripping from his broken nose. As he took it away, he momentarily looked at the blood in his hand. He began to laugh a little as he, one leg at a time and pushing off the floor, rose to his feet.

"Nice one, Jack," he snickered as he turned to reveal his mashed face. "One last hurrah, eh? Well, I think it's time you had that drink."

He reached down, picked up the shot, and walked over to me. Then, with my daughter still holding on tight, he pried my jaw open with one hand and poured the drink in my mouth with the other. I tried to resist, but I was losing energy by the second.

By shoving underneath, he shut my jaw tight. I could feel my mouth becoming numb, like the dentist giving me a shot of Novocain. I growled from its disgusting taste.

Cristina looked up and saw Silva's hand under my chin and threw her arm back.

"Leave my daddy alone!" Because of her height, and by sheer luck, her elbow landed right into his nuts.

Silva's surprise was enough for him to let go of my chin and open his mouth in pain.

Because I hadn't yet swallowed, I spewed the drink right in his face. He took a couple of drunken steps backward.

"My eyes!" he yelled. "You bastard!" He was rubbing his eyes furiously.

My mouth was plenty numb so I knew the toxin would work fast. Within seconds Silva's sight became foggy. He started throwing his arms out in front of him like a blind man without a cane. As he got closer to me, I gave Cristina a flick of my head to tell her to move, then I gave Silva a right cross with my foot. As unsteady as he was, he easily sailed into the wall.

"Ahhhhh!" Silva let out a loud cry. "I had enough of this shit!"

He reached into the small of his back for his gun.

"Cristina, get behind me!" I had to try and protect her while still hanging from the ceiling.

"I'm going to fucking kill you, Jack!"

I stayed quiet as Siva waved his gun out in front of him. Cristina gave out a frightened whimper, which was enough for him to get a shot off in my direction, barely missing the two of us.

I felt a small rock under my foot. Using my shoes like a claw machine in Dave & Buster's, I picked up the stone and tossed it as far as I could to the other side of the room. Silva turned and gave out another shot.

He was starting to stiffen up. The toxins that I spewed on his face and mouth must have been starting to work their voodoo magic.

Just then I heard a door open.

Francine came running in to see what was going on but before she could say a word, just as she turned the corner to the room, Silva got off a third shot. This one hit the mark.

Francine's look of surprise and horror was short-lived, literally. She fell backwards. Silva hit her in the chest, and she was dead before she hit the floor.

CHAPTER TWENTY-TWO

George made it down to the lab in record time. Between the Jolly Ranchers and a Red Bull, the traffic lights were a guessing game for him. They could have been red, or green, or purple for that matter. So, he just slowed as he came upon each of them before traveling through.

As he made his way up the stairs and into his lab, Sanchez was there doing tests on some strands of hair from a missing persons case.

"Hey, George."

"Sanchez. You still got the nose to the grindstone I see."

"Yeah, trying to put together some evidence."

"Well, don't work too hard. The higherups may figure out that they don't really need me."

They both gave a little laugh as George went into

his office. He turned on the light and went directly to the fax machine. There were several pages, all about the case but mostly laymen's information. It wasn't until the last page when he paused. The report read:

> ...there is sufficient evidence...the handcuffs "J D"...no visible serial number...issued to Detective Jim M. Dean...

"Holy shit."

George knew he had to find Jack. He reached in his coat pocket and pulled out his cell phone and dialed Jack's number. It rang until the voicemail picked up, "*Hi, this is my daddy's phone. Please leave him a message.... beep.*"

...beep.

"Hey, Jack, this is George. I need to talk to you man. Call me as soon as you get this."

Maybe he is at his desk or someone there might know where he is, George thought. So, he shut off the light and said goodnight to Sanchez as he headed to his car.

He pulled up to the station just as a tow truck pulled in. When George got out of his car he looked and noticed that the tow was hauling Jack's car into the impound.

"Hey!" George waved down the driver. "Where'd you get this car?"

The driver was a young, Italian looking kid. "The owner of Camille's on the Hill called it in. Said it belonged to a drunk. Once we ran the plate and saw it was a detective's car, we figured we would bring it down here."

"Good thinking. Let me just take a quick look before you put it in the lot."

"Sure. Go ahead."

George didn't know what he was looking for, and Jack's car was not the tidiest, but maybe there was something. Anything.

He poked his head into the passenger's side window. Wrappers, receipts, and Dunkin' coffee cups. The usual stuff. Nothing out of the ordinary.

"What's this?" George asked himself as he cleared the seat of an empty bag of Doritos. Underneath was a half-eaten tuna fish sandwich and a pickle. He picked the plate up off the seat.

George knew that Jack didn't make this himself. The best he's ever seen Jack make was a PB and J, and it was certainly not cut corner to corner.

"Hey, you almost done? I gotta get to an accident over the bridge," the driver called back to George.

Over the bridge?! That's it!

George put the plate back in the safety of the seat. "Yeah, go ahead." He waved to the driver.

As Jack's car pulled away and into the fenced lot, George remembered… Last year he and Jack were finishing up a couple of beers after a softball game against Pawtucket. Jack was complaining of his shoulder, probably from sliding into second, trying to steal. He had asked George to take a ride "over the bridge" into East Providence to a girl's house. He said that she might have some muscle relaxers to get him through the night.

When they pulled up to the house Jack asked George to wait in the car because she is a little "weird" with new people. When a very attractive woman opened the door, George could easily see how she might get weirded out by a lab geek. She went inside, moments later she returned and handed Jack a plate, they hugged, and then the door was closed.

When Jack got back in the car George saw a couple of pills, a pickle, and a tuna sandwich, cut corner to corner, on the plate. They each ate half. Jack even offered one of the pills to George. But not the pickle!

CHAPTER TWENTY-THREE

George had a feeling that time was not on his side. His car was not originally equipped with sirens and lights, but a few years ago he had a friend down at Grasso's in Olneyville make some adjustments. He jumped in and took off down the street a little, and out of earshot of the department, before he turned on the lights and siren.

Just as he flicked the switch under the dash, in an instant the night was lit up like the Fourth of July! It was a bit of a spectacle, but he didn't care. With the siren on, he thought himself to be in the *Ghostbusters* movie.

"Who you gonna call?" he muttered to himself.

HOPING THAT HE REMEMBERED THE HOUSE, HE FLEW OFF THE 195 off ramp to Taunton Ave. There was usually a cop sitting at the gas station waiting for speeders, but tonight he was lucky.

Remembering the street, James (it was easy to remember because it was what his parents wanted to name him), he just had to find the right house. He slowed as he inspected each one for some sign of recollection.

"That's it!" he said as he hit the brakes, making the car chirp.

He pulled into the driveway, remembering the doorway that once held Jack and the gorgeous mystery woman. He had shut his siren and lights off at the beginning of the street, not wanting to alert the entire neighborhood that he was there. He quickly, but quietly, got out of his car and walked up to the door.

Putting his ear to the door, like a five-year-old listening at his parents' bedroom door, he thought he could hear moaning.

George knocked.

The moaning got a little louder.

He knocked again, harder this time.

The moaning turned into a violent, coughing sound.

Fearing for his friend Jack, George kicked in the door like he had seen so many times on SVU. He made a horrendous entrance that assuredly caught the eye of any peeping neighbor, but he didn't care.

But he could not have been any more on time, because laying there on the living room carpet was Rogers in a pool of vomit which he was now choking on. George flew in and rescued this poor soul by giving the Heimlich.

When Rogers started breathing normally, George started slapping him like he was a drunken sailor.

"C'mon! Snap out of it!" George commanded.

Rogers started coming to. "Huh? Hey, why are you slapping me? Why do I feel like I've been throwing up?"

"Well, it wasn't Jiminy Cricket." George pointed to the floor.

"Oh, man. I feel like crap."

"Any idea how you got this way?"

"No. Not really. I remember a beautiful woman. Maybe it was a dream."

"Probably a nightmare instead. Let's get you cleaned up. We have to go and find Jack."

"Jack? We lost Jack? Aw, he was such a nice guy."

Jesus, George thought to himself, this is going to take a couple of minutes.

TIFFANY, WITH A CVS BAG IN HAND, HAD WALKED IN JUST AS George was getting Rogers back onto the couch.

"What's going on here? Who busted my door?" Upon seeing the state of Rogers, "Is he alright?"

"I apologize about the door," George said remorsefully. "My name is George Coffee, I'm a friend of Jack's." Looking at Rogers, "It looks like he's had a slight overdose."

"Jack has mentioned your name before. Oh, and that may be my fault, but I didn't give him much medication to relax him. Must be either allergic or a lightweight. I went to CVS for some Tylenol. I figured that he would wake up with a little headache." Tiffany's facial expression showed some guilt. "Do you know where Jack is?

"Well, don't blame it all on yourself. I may have contributed to his predicament. And to be honest, I'm not sure where Jack is. Been looking for him. Do you have any idea where he could have gone?"

"I wish I did. Said he was going out to do a couple of things but I'm getting worried."

Knowing that his ID was missing, Rogers muttered, "Do you have a computer?"

CHAPTER TWENTY-FOUR

Just then a fourth shot sounded. But this one didn't come from Silva.

From the doorway, behind where Francine's body lay, stood a silhouette. A vaguely familiar one.

"Jack, are you alright?"

Because my mouth was numb, all I could do was to give a childish, "Ah, uh."

My amazement at seeing Rogers was almost overpowered with excitement. He stepped over Francine and walked over to me. He saw that I was handcuffed to the pipe, so he took out his keys to unlock me. My eyes didn't leave his face. It was a face that I would never forget. When he unlocked me, I instinctively gave him a hug.

"Hey, hey, I missed you too buddy," he said coyly.

Rogers had apparently found me at Silva's house in Lincoln by use of a tracking device the Feds had put in their badges a year prior, just in case a circumstance like today happened. In all that had happened here, I completely forgot that I had it.

I let go of my embrace then gave him a couple of pats on the back with a smile.

"Hey, now that's more like it." He laughed.

Looking around he questioned, "What the hell happened here, Jack?"

I began to mutter some of what I'm sure sounded like a drunkard at the Foxy Lady on a Saturday night.

He gave me a queer look. "What the hell is wrong with your voice?"

I squatted down to pick up the shot glass and I wrote the word "poison" in the dirt floor. I pointed to the glass then to my mouth.

Just then another voice entered the room.

"I heard the shots, everyone okay?"

I stood up and gave George an even bigger hug, and this one was returned in form. He was the hippie-hugger type.

"Hey, there you are! Looks like we found you just in time. And it's good to see you as well, little squirt," he said as he bent down to give Cristina a hug.

"It looks like Jack was poisoned. He can't talk," Rogers told George as he held the glass up.

"Can't talk?" George let out a big laugh. "Well, that's good news!"

I gave him a slap on the shoulder and laughed with him.

Just then, behind George, another shadow entered the room.

"Oh, Jack! I've been so worried! Look at you. I have to get you cleaned up. Do you need a doctor?" Tiffany was stumbling over her words, feeling like she couldn't get them out fast enough.

She threw her arms around me as I mumbled, "Ho bot a tun sanich?"

"HEY, SILVA! I THOUGHT HE WAS DEAD!" GEORGE POINTED AT Silva, suddenly seeing him lying on the floor.

"I shot him in the shoulder. It shouldn't have killed him," said Rogers, condemningly.

George walked over to Silva and placed a finger on his neck. "Yup, he's dead alright."

Apparently shooting a guy who is already becoming zombified is lethal.

I looked at Silva. His eyes were wide open.

He wasn't moving a fucking muscle.

EPILOGUE

The next few weeks of rehabilitation were of mixed emotions. George told me about the prints on the handcuffs, which I already knew were Jimmy's. Jimmy was trying to make extra cash for his soon-to-be child, so he must have sold them on the black market. I tried to change the evidence file, but the Feds worked faster than usual.

There was a total of four funerals that I needed to attend. Cristina's mother didn't make it through her surgery, as I suspected. Having to explain to your daughter that her mother was dead is not such a pleasant thing. That was the first one.

The second funeral was just as unbearable: Jimmy's. The turnout was what would be expected of a movie star. In his own right, he was a star. His pregnant wife and the rest of his family, surrounded by a sea of blue.

Francine was the third. I don't think I will ever understand fully what was going through her mind the past few years. Yeah, the sex thing I get, but the Silva affair just didn't make sense. I guess that women like to have choices. No relationship is ever a dead end if you have another to fall on. She was definitely a conflicted soul. I suppose spending some time with Jimmy's wife at Butler Hospital would have done her good.

Finally, I had to go to Silva's funeral, *again*. His wife was in full regalia knowing that this time it was for real. Coincidentally for her, because of the department's screwup with the first one, they were not asking for any of the money back. Amy was at her side wearing a veil so no one could see her face.

It was a very warm day.

And I'm pretty sure I heard a faint, muffled scream.

Eh, could've been the wind.

AFTERWORD

"So, what are you girls talking about?" I inquired playfully as I walked over to the bench with three ice cream cones.

"Nothing, Daddy." Cristina giggled.

I sat next to her. "Here you go Cristina."

"Thank you."

"This one has sprinkles, it must be yours, Auntie Tiffany." Cristina giggled again.

"Thank you, young lady."

We all smiled as we licked our ice cream. It has been a wonderful day here at Six Flags New England in Springfield, Massachusetts.

"Oh, no!" Cristina, in her haste, dropped some chocolate on her shirt.

"Oh, don't worry. We can get it out. Let's go to the ladies room." Tiffany came in a hurry.

The two of them went speedily toward the rest room and left me there without concern.

"These characters." I smiled and shook my head as Porky Pig went drooping by. He was followed shortly by Bugs Bunny. Now, him I crossed my eyes at because he had red paint on his hand and leg. Humph, must have been part of a show, I thought to myself, so I continued with my ice cream.

"All better," Tiffany noted as the two came trotting back. "Did we miss anything?"

"Not a thing," I smiled, just as we heard a violent scream.

Jerry Hutchinson was born and raised in Central Falls, Rhode Island, before joining the Air Force in 1992, then the Rhode Island Air National Guard in 1995. Since then, he has traveled over a great part of the world, aiding global conflicts.

He has attained numerous degrees at the associate level and is currently attending Rhode Island College in the Elementary Education program.

He resides in Cranston, Rhode Island, with his dog Roxy.

www.ingramcontent.com/pod-product-compliance
Lightning Source LLC
LaVergne TN
LVHW010921110826
845149LV00013B/2441

* 9 7 8 1 9 6 5 7 3 3 0 2 8 *